CW01654156

The Godblade

By J. Christopher Tarpey

Cover art by Brian LeBlanc

Back cover art by Ken Kelly

ISBN 978-1-7358982-0-9
Interior illustrations by Ralph Torres
Map of Arginor by Erin Klarer
Cover layout by Michael Greylord
Logo artwork by David "Bulletrider" Göbel

TABLE OF CONTENTS

ARGINOR
Icen
haiklan
Vasik
Waste of En-Faln
Summoner's Pit
Jindoch
Shunned Albrunn
maehlin
Garucu
runefare
Isahin
Vyntane
Red Jewel
Jarion
disna
Tarsul
Arginese Sea
nvala
navordi
Sish
Kynaran
Shar Kut
nitaar
bant

Shallow Sea
Wur
Janak
Barrín
Narav
Duna
Aelbrond
Journ
Bruna River
Wilaken
Yít
Kynara
Sarínuk
Eluvímal
Baruken
Southern Sea

DMR

Chapter I

The Inner Ring

The sharp black peak of Shunned Albrunn stabbed through the flat plain of white clouds like a dagger point through the back. Rænon and his company of ten stood on the rocky wind-torn summit of the Inner Ring, a circle of lesser mountains surrounding the Shunned Mount and the only vantage point from which the shrouded pinnacle of Albrunn could be seen.

They stared awestruck at the flat, unbroken sheet of clouds between them and their objective. "So this is the permamist around Albrunn, eh, Rænon?" asked the short, black-maned axeman from Haiklan. "Unnatural if you ask me. How far you suppose from here?"

"A day and a half, maybe two, Viru," Rænon said flatly.

"Two days!" Viru shot back. "That would be a full day's trek in the Lindoch Range. Why is it double here?"

"What you can't see below these clouds is the Plain of Othra. If we can make our way down this slope of blasted rock and at the same time avoid the Waar'kesh, yes, might be two days."

Viru grumbled at this. He leaned on his axe handle and eyed Rænon. "Then why approach Albrunn from this direction? We could've climbed in from the north, or better yet the west! And the Waar'kesh? Rænon, these are legends. I thought you more skeptical than that."

Rænon shot Viru a poisoned glance. “Viru, not a month ago I watched a horde of sub-demons summon a god from the sea. You suppose I’m not ready for another surprise? Besides, Albrunn is only approachable from the south. This map shows a plateau rising from the plain beneath Farick’s tomb.” Viru attempted to offer argument, but Rænon cut him short. “You like the coin I put there in your pocket? Then close your trap before I take Aarna’s tongs and shut it for good.”

Viru looked back to the others, who were sniggering at his failed parley. They quickly looked away.

Aarna walked up beside Rænon, who hadn’t broken his gaze from the far-off peak. “Maybe we start our descent in the morning, eh?” said the sorcerer-smith who had insisted on joining him on his journey to the Shunned Mount. “The company are tired, they deserve a drink, a little rest. Besides, if Farick is chained dead in his tomb, I’m not sure what the rush is to get there. Care to let me in on your designs?”

“Brakur still wails and tramples over Isahin. What of Farick then?” He paused, reflecting on recent catastrophic events. “Do you remember a legend that Brakur was not always insane? That it created Farick as a guardian? Perhaps, even though our guardian is dead, he has something left to reveal. I’m sorry that’s your answer, but we must go.”

Aarna put his hand on Rænon’s shoulder. “It’s fine, my boy. I suppose the hall of a dead god will be an interesting place regardless.”

Rænon was not accustomed to being called 'boy' but it was permissible from Aarna. He had the grit of ten men, and the old sorcerer-smith had taken precious time since landing back in Arginor to teach Rænon the fading art of the pyre-forge at the ancient smithy in Maehlin.

"Yes, interesting to say the least, old man," he smiled. "Let's get a fire going."

Not long ago Rænon journeyed to Vyntane. His adventures there were drastically different from what he expected, culminating in his slaying of the degenerate King Tavrik who loosed the insane god Brakur upon the unsuspecting populace. Upon Rænon's return to his homeland, Hyrk, the ruler of Aelbrond, appointed him to Guard Command. Rænon was hesitant to take the position, but accepted. Hyrk was a student of the prose of Farick and admirer of "Aelbrond's Underlord" as he called him. Upon hearing Rænon's tale from Vyntane he immediately commissioned him to seek Farick's tomb, as well as hire the sellswords of his choosing to deal with any threats the mountains had on offer.

Among those Rænon hired were three hardmen named Murk, Balan and Vaski, who were Guards of Lourn from the east. Balan went through months of guard training with Rænon as an adolescent before going east to Lourn, while Rænon remained in Maehlin for years as a smith and combat trainer. All four had taken oaths. These men he trusted.

Four more hailed from the north in Haiklan: two axemen

called Viru and Dyshlan from the port of Lindoch, and two women, Kiv and Tafala, who were archers from the Waste of En-Faln, northeast of Aelbrond. They asked more money than Rænon wanted to pay, but when he saw both archers put an arrow in a fowl's head from a hundred yards, he deemed them worth the extra coin.

Then there were the two killers from Disna, the sorcery-ridden capital of Tarsul. Rænon wasn't sure if they were mercenaries, sorcerers, or torturers, but, in an attempt to win his favor, he watched both men *run* up an unscalable tower in Disna and compel the Arhai cultists to hand over the map to Farick's tomb. They descended as effortlessly as they went up and handed Rænon the much-guarded map, now with the fresh blood of the cult's guards smeared across the Arginese Sea.

These two killers spoke the Tarsulean tongue, a language Rænon never learned. But the two slender, light-eyed and leather-clad assassins responded to the names Tahv and Kehd, as well as Rænon's crude gesturing.

Rænon was clad in his usual attire, a coat of bear fur held fast by steel ringlets around his sinewed arms with chain mail enforced shoulders. He bore his pyre-forged sword Pitkeeper on his back, and his axe and large knife were hung on either side of his belt.

The archers from Haiklan were ill-dressed for the journey. Their pale legs were bare beneath the segmented fur-bound steel lames that covered their asses and waists, and each wore short fur coats loosely tied together in front and often revealing one or both teardrop-shaped breasts. He knew those from Haiklan were not a shy people, but baring their skin in this altitude and temperature impressed him. The archers' fur boots were fitted with short steel spikes on the toe and under the sole, so they clanked while climbing behind him and Aarna, who bore his pyre-forged helm and light hammered steel cuirass.

The axemen, in true Haiklan custom, wielded broad, double-bit war axes. They wore bleached white furs to blend with their native frostland, and their dark hair was tied back with fine silver bands.

The company of eleven were around the fire singing, passing two horns of strong ale. Even Rænon, who was always in his head, found it hard to resist. The months since his ordeal on Isahin had been long and surreal. His entire life he wondered if the gods existed. Now that he had seen one, he wished that they didn't. His grey eyes shone bright in the fire as he stared into the blaze... then he pushed the thoughts away, joining in for the chorus of "Ragban's Curse."

Above the clouds the air was still. Their voices rang out to the clear night sky and down the crags below. One by one their voices dropped out 'til there was only one faithful crooner left following his bardic duty, sending his father's songs out to the night. Rænon felt himself drifting off.

Suddenly Rænon shot up. The sound of a gasp that wanted to be a scream was one he recognized. A man in red boiled leather armor stood over Viru, slowly taking the swordpoint out of his neck.

In one quick motion Rænon unsheathed Pitkeeper and swung it at Viru's killer, taking him in the knee and sending him screaming to the ground. This woke the company. Rænon grabbed the axe from his belt. Cautious of saving the edge of his weapon, he hit the attacker squarely with the butt of it, shattering his face and silencing him forever.

More men crested the summit quickly. None carried torches, making it difficult to tell how many were coming up out of the darkness. They bore the red armor of Kynara. Rænon clenched his jaw, his vision became a tunnel. He remembered the prose of Farick: *"The Armor of Ire is brittle, if not tempered."* He fought down the primal urge to lose himself in bloodshed.

The first wave approached Rænon as he stood in front of his company. He could hear Kiv and Tafala's bowstrings stretch back and creak before letting loose. The first two Kynarans fell, each taking an arrow in the face. The next four fanned out and attacked at the flanks. Rænon found his target in the center of the fray. This was a big man, a half foot taller than Rænon, which meant he was more than seven feet. The straw-haired Kynaran held a short sword in each hand. His first strike from his right hand was aimed at Rænon's head, the second from his left arm tried to come down and surprise Rænon from his prone position. Instead, Rænon drew up Pitkeeper fast to send his attacker's blades in a course down to the dirt. Now the Kynaran brought both his swords upward at Rænon's neck. He dodged them but felt their wind as they passed. *Too close,* he thought. The big Kynaran put too much into this maneuver though, and brought his body around far enough for Rænon to kick him back and force him to drop one of his swords in order to catch himself on the ground.

Rænon seized this opportunity and brought Pitkeeper down onto his attacker's red helm. It bit into the thin steel and a stream of blood trickled down onto the Kynaran's forehead. Dazed, and blind for all the blood, the assailant in red lunged straight at Rænon. His charge was not quick enough, for Rænon stepped aside easily and plunged his longsword into the Kynaran's back as he passed.

Quickly, two more warriors stepped in as Rænon took Pitkeeper from the back of the big man. They were smaller but attacked from both sides. Each wore a cylindrical helm that covered their face but for two small slits for vision. They rushed in at Rænon. His only move was to jump toward one man and let the other catch up once he landed. As he leaped, he found the weakness in the Kynarans' boiled leather armor. He plunged the point of his blade in between the shoulder piece and neck plate. The warrior gurgled and fell clutching his throat. The other one still came rushing toward Rænon, sword cocked behind his head. The Aelbronder had enough time to block this descending arc. While holding his attacker's sword aloft on Pitkeeper's guard, he took the Kynaran's dagger from his own belt, and with an uppercut sent the dagger through the man's chin and into his brain. Rænon dropped the dagger and the man.

He looked upon the scene. Aside from Viru, none of his company had fallen. He had chosen them well. Aarna was trading blows with one of the last of the band of attackers. A lofty downward swing put Aarna on his knee, holding the descending blade back on his cross guard. Quickly Aarna turned the Kynaran's steel towards the ground and brought his own blade up into the man's leg. The Kynaran shrieked and dropped his sword and clutched his wound with both hands. Blood gushed from between his fingers. The second strike from Aarna sent his head rolling off the mountainside and into to the mist.

There were three more approaching the band from below. These were not Kynarans. They wore all black, and their skin was pale as the moons, but tracked with black veins. Their faces were scribed with black ink, runes or symbols Rænon couldn't recognize. Where other men's eyes were white, theirs were black. The pupils were a horrible crimson. They wore no metal and wielded no metal. Chiseled obsidian plates covered their shoulders and chests and they brandished obsidian double-bit axes. The pair reminded Rænon of the cult, The Starless Night, he encountered at Vyntane and their hatred for steel.

Again Kiv and Tafala shot their arrows past each side of Rænon, attempting to take the flanking attackers and leave the middle one for him. Their arrows found their targets, striking each in the chest between their chiseled armor plating, but still they came forward, hissing and shrieking through jagged teeth. The sound sent a shiver through the members of the company. It was a piercing, unnatural sound. As any human should have fallen from an arrow through the chest, they could only imagine what these beings were.

Vaski and Murk stepped in front of the archers and met the two fiends with heavy axe blows. Their blades clashed above their heads and the obsidian axes sparked against the cold Maehlish steel. Vaski swung his axe furiously as the rune-marked assailant displayed uncanny agility for his size and was able to dodge each blow. Finally Vaski found a pattern in his movement and his next swing landed in the neck. The attacker fell to the ground croaking, his dark blood leaving him. Balan turned around to see Murk finding his mark as well, swinging through the haft of the obsidian axe and then burying the backspike of his own weapon into the red-eyed one's chest. Blood sprayed fountain-like as he met the ground twitching.

Rænon waited for the last one to approach. *Was this a soldier?* He was walking ahead slowly. Being outnumbered ten to one, he must know his time was short.

Rænon held his arm out to the others as a signal to let this last one attack him directly. Instead of the hewn armor, this one wore a long black hooded robe. It lifted the dark veil with its hands, human-like though hideously tipped with long black claws. This one was tall and thin, even weak looking. Its aspect seemed less demonic than the other two though certainly it was not a man. Its skin was wan and varicose, and its eyes shone yellow and reptile-like in the fire.

The robed one stared at Rænon, then smiled through jagged pointed teeth. "Nishu ag Nitaar, felu tyn nat Arhai." It chucked these words at Rænon. They were guttural, an utterly alien speech. Again, this time yelling, "Nishu ag Nitaar, felu tyn NAT Arhai!"

With this it charged at Rænon, pulling a long black axe out from behind its back and hefting it above its head.

Rænon held Pitkeeper at his side until the last moment, then he followed the axe down with his sword and held it there in the dirt. The one in black hissed a noise at Rænon as he kept the stone axe pinned to the ground. Rænon then gave the creature a left cross which shattered its yellow teeth and sent it back on the ground without its weapon. The one in black crawled back from Rænon on its elbows, shuffling away from the Aelbronder who was now gripping Pitkeeper tightly and holding the thing's gaze as he walked forward.

"Rrrrraaaaaaanon." The thing spat his name through pieces of teeth and black blood. "Brakur knows you, he saw you in a thousand dreams, he seeeeees you now."

"Good, I've seen Brakur too, an insane god with an army of hairless goats." He smiled back and put Pitkeeper's point at the neck of this last survivor.

"Not goats anymore," it laughed, drooling black blood. "Nishu ag Nitaar, felu tyn nat Arhai!" Then an arrow hit the thing between the eyes. Rænon looked back to see Tafala letting her bow down, a disgusted look on her face.

"I was not done with him yet," Rænon said as he sheathed Pitkeeper.

"I couldn't look at it anymore," she said as she looked on Rænon with remorse. "I am sorry, but that phrase… it is notorious in the texts of Arhai. I studied them on a cursed trip to Navordi.

These pale ones in black are from Nitaar."

Rænon still stared at the unwholesome visage, the arrow placed perfectly between its xanthous eyes. He cocked his head back at Tafala. "And what does it mean?"

She looked at him gravely. *"Up from Nitaar, the Arhai send thousands."*

"Thousands of these things? I don't see a problem there, half the Guards of Lourn would make a morning out of it."

Tafala shook her head, trembling as she spoke. "Not these, this is a demon-priest. The texts say thousands of *Adyrtun, the clawed and fanged,* like these other two." She kicked the pale one with the head barely connected. "Nitaar must be gaining influence over Kynara. They will seek to join their armies to come against Aelbrond. Right now Haiklan, Tarsul, Lanak, and The Western Isles all remain loyal only to themselves, but soon they'll have to stand together against Kynara and the black influence of Ill-Nitaar, or succumb to it."

Rænon looked unconvinced. "And what does Nitaar want? What does Brakur want?"

"Brakur wants to die, Nitaar wants to live forever," she said solemnly.

"Maniacs, all," Rænon chuckled to himself. "More words from the texts?" he said sarcastically.

"Yes." Tafala walked back to Kiv, who was staring into the fire, holding tight the Ylar pendant which hung between her breasts.

Rænon looked to Aarna. "Kynara and Nitaar allied. Makes some sense, don't you think? Kynara is likely overrun with these demon priests and the land has been slipping into fanaticism for years. Men that rode with my father say he was killed by a black band with pale skin and yellow eyes, struck by a stone blade and arrows. Perhaps I am wrong to blame the whole of Kynara, but they accept Nitaar with open arms. This cult grows too large."

Aarna wiped the blood from his blade in an unworried fashion. He took the wineskin from his belt and drained it. "Aye, this has been on my mind since we left Isahin… the Cult of Arhai has spread out like a plague from Nitaar. Its influence and promise of eternity have infected Tarsul and Isahin, as you know, and now certainly Kynara's red shores. They're organized, they know we are here and where we are going, I suggest we keep moving."

Rænon announced to his company, "Quickly take what you like from the dead. We must bury Viru here, but save his sword and his heart. I will pyre-forge them for his sons when we return."

Chapter II

The Survivor of Vyntane

Narila's hand traced a gentle circle over the top of the crouching demon's head. The onion-skinned, hairless creature knelt in front of her as she lay back, in her way, across the carved throne of ebon rock in the hall under the ruins of the Iron Castle. Raven hair fell over her shoulders but could do nothing to hide her massive, heavy breasts. She resisted wearing clothes, even in the damp, cool, throne room where there was no one to admire her buxom form but the uninterested, degenerated spawn of The Starless Night.

Her eyes were now of different colors; one had remained dark brown and the other was now the palest grey. Her face had two scars, one around her now light eye and the other on her forehead. They were freshly healed but ruined the symmetrical beauty of the face in her previous life as Tavrik's favorite concubine. She still retained an undeniable comeliness.

Above the throne, the rotting head of Suut stood placed atop an obsidian pike, the archdemon's white flesh putrefying, falling off the skull and filling the hall with the noxious stench of a dead demon.

On the other side of the throne, opposite Narila's pet, stood a long table with a large map of Arginor and Nitaar laid out across it. She stared at the map venomously. "My riders have left Navordi for Shunned Albrunn, and if they don't bring me Rænon's head then I will feed them to you. How does that sound?" The sub-demon growled slightly. She slapped its head where moments earlier she had caressed. "I said, how does that sound?" Her pet growled louder. The other Starless Night in the throne room clacked the stone flags with their hooves, screamed their high-pitched wails into the hall and above to the ruined castle.

After the caterwauling ceased there was a brief silence, then the hall, the ruins, Vyntane itself began to tremble. Stones loosed from the ceiling and broke apart on the throne room floor right in front of Narila, though she was unmoved, even annoyed. "Brakur still tramples atop Isahin, but I remain here, sequestered as his keeper. I will find a use for the rest of you... perhaps with your efforts we can wake Brakur long enough to hear reason." The small group of demon acolytes began their screeching again, filling the hall with sickening song.

Chapter III

Othra

The company, now of ten, made their way down the rim of the Inner Ring and into the permamist. It was the Sun Season and the snow was only a crust over the granite rocks. The mist grew thick with their descent. Even with the light of their torches, visibility became worse until each man lost the next in line and communication had to be constant. Rænon hoped to reach the plain by first light. That way, it would be of no consequence that they couldn't see their own hands for the fog.

Kiv followed right behind Rænon, the other eight trekked after them, with Tafala in the back should another surprise come from behind that required the archer's quick precision.

"So, how long has it been since anyone has laid eyes on Albrunn?" Kiv questioned Rænon, keeping an arrow nocked, trying to keep his voice right in front of her as they climbed down.

"Ages, who knows? If the legends are true, and I doubt they are, no one has approached the Shunned Mount since dead Farick was sealed inside and the Waar'kesh were brought up to guard it."

Kiv kept prying. "Brought up? You mean from the Summoner's Pit? Who wants it guarded?"

"The legend says a sorcerer from Ill-Nitaar summoned them. I don't know why they fear Farick, why they want to bring Brakur out of his dreams, as they say. Theology confuses me. Maybe 'confuses' is the wrong word—it *irritates* me."

A smile broke across Kiv's face. "I can't keep it straight myself. I heard Tafala speaking to you about the Arhai. If Brakur wants to die and the cult wants eternity, do you think the Arhai are possibly using Brakur for their ends?"

The thought hadn't occurred to Rænon. "Maybe. I always assumed because Nitaar was an evil place, naturally they would worship an insane god. Perhaps they aim to use the god in its weakened state… I hope Albrunn will shine light on this. Something pulls me there."

"And if Brakur dies, what will become of us, of Arginor? If the Insane God is the first god, the creator, will it unmake the world?"

"More legends, but if Brakur is so old, so maddened by eternity that it forgot it made the world in its youth, maybe there are other truths that that are hidden from it. I try not to think of such things. After all, what can I do? If a god wants to die, what could I do to stop it?" Under his breath he added, "Maybe I should aid it." Rænon didn't want to sound cynical to his sellswords, but he grew tired of talk of gods and their plans.

Kiv kept at him. "And the Waar'kesh, there are no tales of them in Maehlin?"

"There are plenty," Rænon replied, "but again I doubt the legends. Some say they are blind, from a place where eyes and legs are not needed."

"If they are blind, and cannot walk, I'm not too worried!"

Balan offered from somewhere down the line of climbers.

"They may not need eyes to see, but if they are put here to be a threat, then we must assume they are one," Aarna declared. He sounded ancient to the young Guard of Lourn.

The clouds remained thick all through the night and into the early morn. The sun barely penetrated the mist at all and their way was becoming even more obscured as the band climbed down the Inner Ring. It was now mid-morning, but the permamist had made the light dim and lavender-hued like the sundown before a storm.

The landscape was changing. This was made clear to Rænon by the nature of rocks they were climbing down. The shale was looser, with small patches of heather beginning to appear between the boulders. He hoped to reach the plain and the base of Albrunn by nightfall, but a thought occurred to him: if the sun is truly blotted out under the permamist, then nightfall might not be an issue for them. Silently, he hoped they brought enough torches.

He could hear those in his company behind him becoming tired, taking slower steps and grunting over the small obstacles in the thick cloud. He presumed it was close to noon, but it was impossible to tell, for they were so far down the mountain that the mist had obscured the sun. All was a dark grey morass for the climbers.

Finally, after another hour descending through the ashen pall, the mist started to clear. Stretching out before them was an uncanny vista.

Less than a few hundred feet down was the plain of Othra. As each climber descended out of the mist they could see for miles across the plain. From their high vantage point one could follow the walls of the Inner Ring which formed the border of the plain in each direction until it was lost to the horizon. In the center of their view, though miles away, was the base of Shunned Albrunn.

Tafala, at the back of the line, was the last to reach the bottom. Now they all stood together in a slow-moving rivulet. A strange purple sunlight lit the landscape. It refracted through the mist into a lavender shade. The perma-fog hung above them not a bowshot away, a flat sky of mist, floating not quite motionless, but still enough to create a feeling of unease in one who stared at it too long.

The Plain of Othra was a cell of clear air, a vast circular expanse, with the walls of the Inner Ring forming a border. They could see clear across the plain to their goal, the rocky base of Albrunn, which rose up until the weird sky of Othra severed it.

The vegetation here was as strange as the light. The floor was spongy, thick with lichens or a tightly clustered and cropped grass. No trees dotted the landscape, but tall plants, stalky and angular, grew in small groups, each group being a different color: gold or azure or blazing crimson. Instead of leaves they had long, brightly-colored thorns which stood out in contrast to the shade of the stalk from which it grew.

As a boy in Lindoch, Rænon had seen a giant glass cage in

the city's market. It was filled with sea water and in it swam the abominations pulled up from the abyssal trenches of the Arginese. He felt as though they were in one of these cages now.

No life appeared as they walked toward the center of the Ring and the base of Albrunn beyond. Their footsteps were almost silent on the forgiving turf. Large, sharp rocks began jutting out from the soft ground, finally grouping together in a way that forced the company to choose a direction through the labyrinth.

"Should we stick together, Rænon?" Aarna questioned.

"Aye, we need everyone together if things don't stay this quiet."

The base of Albrunn had become so large in their horizon that it dominated their vision. The walls of the Inner Ring were now lost to them except to their backs.

Albrunn is a mountain on a mountain, Rænon thought to himself. The surreal environment made him wonder if the laws of nature were somehow different on this plain with the weird purple light and alien plant life. His thoughts turned back to the glass cage he saw as a boy.

Something moved under his boot. Quickly Rænon stepped aside and saw a slithering shape embossed under the spongy turf. It was at least ten feet long and thick as his arm. Without thinking he put Pitkeeper where he guessed its head would be and stabbed down through the turf. The thing convulsed, sending a sickening vibration through his blade and up into his arm that made him shudder, but he wouldn't relent his grip. Then, with a snap, the thing ripped through the turf from its opposite end. The tail terminated in a single spike, as long as a dagger, protruding out of a fleshy pink worm. Rænon kept his sword in what he wagered was the head. The spike darted toward him, doubling over the creature's own body in a final defiance of its slayer, but he dodged with catlike agility. The thing went still. Rænon lifted his sword, ripping the remaining portion of the worm-thing out from under the soft green turf, and held it up so that the company could see.

"Is that a Waar'kesh?" Kiv asked, putting down her bow that was trained on the worm.

"I hope so," Rænon said with a smile. "If these are all our troubles, I will settle for it. This thing has no eyes, almost no teeth, only a tail to watch out for." He flung its head from his blade. It fell with a deadened thump. Blue-black blood poured out from the wound.

But there was a green liquid coming out of its tail spike. A small amount, but what was there burned through the turf, causing light wisps of smoke to rise from the small incendiary pool.

"A poisoned tail," Aarna observed.

Again Rænon ordered the company to stay in a line, with one archer at the front and another at the back should another worm approach them from the rear. He kept Kiv with him at the front.

They kept their pace through the rock walls. Most kept their gaze at the ground, looking for movement under the turf. The rock walls barely turned and formed a mostly straight path to the base of Albrunn. The way was narrow but they never shot off in another direction. Always the Shunned Mount remained in front of them.

Rænon was the first to hear the high-pitched ringing. "Quiet!" he said. The company stood still, listened, then eyed him as if he were overly cautious.

Silence.

Tavh and Kedh each shot up either side of the rock wall and looked out over the expanse. Tavh held out his hand to Rænon and counted the space between his outstretched fingers, then made a movement with his hand like the slithering of a snake. Rænon realized immediately what the Tarsulean meant. They were in the eroded channels of an ancient riverbed. Vaski gripped his axe so tightly the company could hear his hands rubbing back and forth on the hardoak handle, his palms sanding the haft. Again came the noise, higher this time, even torturous. It stung their ears with a novel, alien sound.

Now everyone stood still in the line. The tall rocks blocked their view so that only a sliver of the permamist sky could be seen hanging motionless above them.

Just then, something directly above them flew below the permamist and back up again, a dark thing against the light grey sky. Rænon heard Kiv's bowstring creak. It was a sound he was beginning to love. Kiv loosed a black arrow ahead of where the thing broke through the clouds, anticipating its direction. For a moment there was silence.

Once again the high-pitched sound broke the still. This time, not right below the clouds but right above their heads, a dark, winged thing shot over their sliver of ground between the rock walls.

"Get on top of the rocks," Rænon ordered. Even before he could finish his sentence, everyone had joined Tavh and Kedh atop the walls. They could see the thing only for a few seconds before it speedily flew back up into the mist on translucent, rapidly beating wings. "Ylar's tits! How can something so big move so fast?" Rænon said puzzledly. Kiv and Tafala each nocked arrows. The rest of the company kept their gaze on the strange sky, every hand gripping a blade.

Now from behind they heard, unaccompanied by high-pitched ringing, the hum of beating wings. Not ten yards away a creature hovered above the group. They saw an eyeless face covered in a dozen or so white mushroom-shaped growths. Under these horrible fungi-like growths hung a gaping mouth, ravening, lined with rows of narrow fangs contained within a hoary fleshed mouth. The creature was the size of three horses, its hide dark green but for a patch of short vermillion tentacles on its underside and four slightly opaque wings that beat with a sickening whir. Its skin seemed to be hard, like an insect's chitin, and at its end there was a cluster of dark spikes.

Again Tafala, acting without Rænon's order, loosed her arrow at the thing. Her shot deflected off its exo-armor. They heard a cry that came from The Pit itself. So loud and hellish was the caterwauling, it was hard for the warriors to fight the urge to drop their weapons and shield their ears, to rake at them, to scream themselves hoarse and run back to the walls of the Inner Ring, back to their taverns and campfires and brothels.

The thing ceased its shrieking, then brought its back end around like a hornet and shot one of its tail spikes at Dyshlan. It flew unerringly like a dart. He had no chance of dodging.

The dark spike found its target in his upper leg. At first it had the effect one would expect of a mundane arrow hitting a fleshy target, but then, in an unnatural way, the spike seemed to burrow farther into his leg. Dyshlan screamed for Ylar. He screamed and tried in vain to pull at the spearhead-sized spike that was now tunneling deeper inside him. Within seconds the spike was all the way inside the Haiklaner's leg. Acting with a will of its own, it moved upward into the thigh as the man wailed. Rænon kept an eye on the still-hovering abomination, making sure that it stayed where it was; it did. It seemed to be waiting for some reason. Perhaps it expected the company to abandon Dyshlan so it could feed on its victim. If that were so, it would wait forever, for they wouldn't leave him.

Under Dyshlan's skin the living spike crawled, still heading upwards, over his ribcage and within moments into his neck. Dyshlan looked at Murk gravely. *"Kill me..."* he groaned, spitting blood as the spike headed northward. Murk drove his dagger into Dyshlan's heart as an act of mercy, but it didn't bring the anticipated death. Still Dyshlan looked upon the company in horror, eyes wide with awareness as the living spike burrowed into the man's brain.

Murk retrieved the dagger and once more plunged it into his heart, but again Dyshlan's eyes were those of a man fully awake and conscious.

This time the Haiklaner took the dagger out of his own heart and handed it back to Murk, who accepted it in shock. He pushed aside the men holding him up and walked toward the hovering thing. Rænon called to him, "Dyshlan! What are you doing!" Yet the Haiklaner did not halt.

Once he was beside the thing, he turned around to face the company again. His eyes still held the horror of his should-be death, his will overridden somehow. Dyshlan looked as if he stared into an eternal abyss. The winged thing lowered for the axeman to climb onto its back. They all looked on with horror as the abomination now had a rider with eyes to see.

The Waar'kesh! I've doomed these men, Rænon thought to himself.

Now the Waar'kesh with its rider rose above the group. Behind it another shape descended from the permamist.

"More of them, let's move!" yelled Balan.

"Hold on!" Rænon ordered. "We can't leave one of our own to this fate."

"You want to die here, Rænon?" Balan shouted back at him.

"Here is as good a place as any." Rænon smiled nihilistically and ran toward the Waar'kesh, his axe in his right hand. The Waar'kesh reeled and aimed its spiked abdomen at him, but it was not quick enough. Rænon threw his axe into the soft, tentacled underbelly of the thing, which erupted with a yellow ichor. The Waar'kesh and its newly acquired eyes fell towards the earth. The whole company charged the fallen fiend, hacking at the shrieking abomination until it ceased twitching. Dyshlan stood, now on broken legs from the fall, still living in some nightmare. Tafala sent an arrow between his eyes, which now finally and mercifully went vacant. Rænon looked upon her approvingly. With this act she had partially redeemed herself, he thought.

The second Waar'kesh was now right upon them. This one carried an ancient rider, only a skeleton, still bearing the helm and armor of ancient Aelbrond. In its skull burned the tormented eyes of a will undermined for centuries. As the Waar'kesh lowered, it poised its spiked tail at the company. Tahv and Kehd leaped and attacked it from either side, each slashing at the tentacled belly of the Waar'kesh with their daggers. It fell, and the company took pleasure in its high-pitched screams as they dismembered it.

Rænon seized the long-dead Aelbronder and grabbed the ancient rider's spine. He palmed the skull with his other hand and crushed it, leaving only the black leathery spike squirming in his fist. He skewered it on Pitkeeper and watched as the black sluggish thing still tried to make its way down the blade towards Rænon's hand.

"How about we burn these things and get moving?"

Chapter IV

Into the Shunned Mount

The company was nearing Albrunn's base. Sprinting on top of the rock channels of the ancient riverbed, Rænon led the line while keeping a close watch above. No more dark shapes descended. As he ran he could feel the yellow ichor of the Waar'kesh drip from his axe blade onto his leg. The burning was only an annoyance at first but became searing by the time they reached the base of Albrunn. Tahv and Kehd were much worse off, for they were covered in the gruesome substance from their ordeal with the eyeless hornets of Othra.

As they stood catching their breath at the base of the Shunned Mount, Rænon noticed the xanthous splotches covering the Tarsuleans from head to boot. He walked over to them and asked, "Your skin, does it burn?" Rænon pointed to the spot on his leg which was a stain of yellow with a red ring around it. Kehd understood him and nodded stoically. Rænon could see they were in pain.

A trickle of water ran down the mountainside. This was the Sun Season, so Albrunn's peak was barren of snow. The melted snow crystals were the source of the small stream that they stood in that morning when they descended the Inner Ring.

"The snowmelt must be what formed these channels. We're lucky it's the Sun Season," offered Aarna, always the optimist.

Rænon cupped his hands and let some water from the sloping granite fill them. He sniffed it suspiciously, wary of being taken by another of Othra's venoms. He sipped from it slowly at first, then as he realized his thirst, he drank greedily. The others followed suit.

But just as he splashed some of the water onto the caustic wound on his leg, it burned as if he had poured hot oil on it. "The hell!" Rænon said aloud, louder than he wanted to.

He rubbed the yellowish stain on his leg and the skin came off in his hand, leaving a red bleeding wound. He looked up at Tahv and Kehd. They were splashing themselves with the water as well. Immediately they came to the same conclusion that he did and screamed their own blasphemies to Tarsulean gods.

The horror came as they tried to dry their faces, which had been mostly covered with the yellow blood of the Waar'kesh. The natural instinct to relieve their pain with the cold water made things worse.

Their faces came off in *one piece.*

Each of them screamed into the other's skinless visage, their now lidless eyes unable to shut out the terror of the horrible vicissitude. The company looked on in shock as the Tarsuleans were overcome by pain both physical and metaphysical.

Balan, Murk and Vaski, hardened Guards of Lourn, went pale. All three men had to look away. Kiv and Tafala turned their backs, almost getting sick from the scene. The Tarsuleans' screams persisted. Unable to find relief, or to even shut their eyes, both men were now becoming desperately suicidal.

Aarna, readying his sword to deliver peace to the howling men, was held back by Rænon's corded arm. He pointed in the distance as two more Waar'kesh came screaming down from the permamist. "Steel yourselves!" Rænon ordered. The company turned their eyes to Othra's firmament and saw the pair of Waar'kesh rapidly descend. An ancient skeletal rider straddled each, their eyes aglow with reluctant vassalhood.

Tavh and Kehd, even in their most desperate moment, realized their opportunity to both save the band and die with their honor. Each of them drew their long flame-shaped daggers and ran howling at the descending Waar'kesh.

They were met almost instantly as the winged monstrosities hovered right above the ground, grappling the Tarsuleans with their fleshy red tentacles. Kehd slashed through the softer appendages. He seemed to be overcoming the thing until the Waar'kesh quickly opened its wide jaws, flew back a few paces and took his head effortlessly, swallowing it whole.

Tavh wildly stabbed into the Waar'kesh's softer underside. His hacking succeeded in doing sufficient harm to the monster that the whirring of its wings ceased and it dropped to the ground. Its grating shrill cry rang out.

Tavh killed the rider quickly, smashing his skull and finally releasing him from his terrestrial bondage. Still howling from the pain of his missing face as well as the joy of battle, he plunged his dagger deep into the Waar'kesh until his arm was buried up to the elbow in its burning ichor. Before Tavh had a chance to withdraw his blade, the remaining Waar'kesh flew over quickly, and took the head from him as well.

Rænon, again using his throwing axe to keep himself at a distance from the abomination, found his mark in the crimson underside of the thing. Now it fell the short distance to the ground but, alas, oriented itself in such a way that enabled it to shoot its dark slugs at the Aelbronder. Rænon anticipated them this time and knocked the flying spike away with Pitkeeper. Again the Waar'kesh, with its last bit of strength, hurled another spike. With his sword Rænon deflected it, this time slicing the thing in half with the edge.

He walked up calmly to the dying fiend and its ancient rider. This one bore the obsidian armor of Ill-Nitaar, so he left it to its fate, assuming the ragged skeleton had played a part in the original conspiracy to bring the Waar'kesh up from The Pit and to Albrunn.

The thing gnashed at the Aelbronder with its long fangs. Rænon waited for the right moment. While its mouth was wide open he shoved Pitkeeper up into its head, intending to pierce the thing's brain. The Waar'kesh finally was still. The skeletal Nitaarian rider lay trapped under the thing, his half-dead eyes following Rænon as he walked back towards what was left of the company.

Now they were seven.

"It's time to get up this damned mount before I lose any more of you to it." Rænon felt pangs of guilt for bringing these fighters to such a place. Even though he knew each of them would loathe a bed-death, this was a bad place to die.

Twenty or so paces from the trickling ice melt began a series of rough-hewn steps leading up the white and black speckled rock face. Each step was only large enough for one foot. Climbing would be precarious.

Rænon led, this time leaving Aarna right behind him, with the archers in the middle and the three Guards of Lourn in the back.

The slope was at such an angle one could lean toward the rock face and stand securely, but at some intervals the face became almost vertical and forced one to choose the next move carefully. The footholds were carved in such a way that, once committed, a step was difficult to take back.

Rænon's climb was made easier by his refusal to wear much armor. His long, leather *teru* and boots kept him agile and his load light. The archers' cleated boots clung fast to the granite and they clinked securely behind him and Aarna. In the back of the line the Guards of Lourn were enjoying the view of the archers while they had it, though they struggled under the burden of their steel and heavy iron-enforced boots.

In an hour they had climbed the few hundred lengths to the permamist. The weird lavender light had dulled throughout the day. As Rænon was level with the flat base of the strange clouds he looked below to the Plain of Othra. He spied its ancient channeled riverbed leading out to the short turf and brightly colored copses of thorny-stalked bushes. He hoped there was a way back to the Inner

Ring from inside Albrunn so that he would not have to see it again.

Soon they were all above the clear air and into the permamist. Rænon called down the line, "Everyone still on the wall?"

"Aye" called the archers.

Rænon heard the Aelbronders in the back grunt in reply.

"Rænon, you hear that?" Aarna whispered.

"It was Balan in the back, he is whining."

"No, listen."

Then Rænon heard what he meant… "The Waar'kesh—move it!"

Synchronized, the company accelerated up the rock face of Albrunn. The incline was becoming less vertical and now they could start to run up the gradual incline. Behind him, Rænon could hear Aarna keeping up on his heels, the light-footed clink of the archers' cleated boots close behind, the Guards in the back shuffling up the loose boulders. Then came the piercing shrill of the Waar'kesh somewhere close in the thick permamist.

Suddenly, as Rænon anticipated another step in the dense mist, he overshot his stride and lunged forward onto a flat carved ledge. Behind him, Aarna stumbled. Rænon grabbed him by the arm and helped him ready for the flat floor which appeared suddenly out of the fog. The archers and the Guards of Lourn shot out of the mist and onto the ledge with arrows nocked and swords drawn, eyes down into the cloud, waiting for the Waar'kesh to shoot out of their realm and into Aelbrond's sacred air.

Rænon walked across the igneous floor towards the face of Albrunn. He looked back at the company, the six of them framed against the rugged peaks of The Inner Ring in the distance with the flat sheet of mist between them, and he realized he was standing near Shunned Albrunn's summit. The range in the distance was his vantage point the day before.

"Stay there," he called back to the band. Again he heard the bowstrings creak. *I would keep these two forever,* he thought to himself.

Carved out of the igneous rock was an arched and chiseled door. He pushed on it hard, not really expecting it to move. It didn't.

He looked behind him and saw the entire company standing close by. "I said to stand back."

"And wait for the Waar'kesh?" Balan shot sarcastically. Rænon noted the insolence in his tone.

Aarna, noticing the brewing animosity between the two men, said quickly, "The door is jointed, look." He brought their attention to the intersecting lines which cut the door in half lengthwise from the top of the arch to the floor. Another carved line stretched across the door horizontally met the longer line the middle. At the nexus was an inlaid circular brass plate, flat against the granite, engraved with the ancient language of Aelbrond.

"The tombdoor of Farick," Rænon said while tracing his fingers over the ancient engravings.

"What does it say?" Kiv questioned.

"In another time," Rænon said quietly.

He reached into a pocket inside his bear fur. When he pulled out his fist, it now bore a spiked knuckler.

Before the company could stand aside, Rænon crouched a bit, pivoted quickly on his back foot, and put his body into a right blow directly into the brass plate bearing old Aelbrond's runes.

The plate dented and the granite crumbled around it, leaving its edges slightly turned outward. Again he struck the plate. This time as Rænon withdrew his arm the spiked knuckler took the plate with it. He smiled, whipped his fist down to fling the plate from it.

Where the plate had been, now a circular aperture into the rock door reached back into the darkness. Rænon stuck Pitkeeper into the aperture, all the way to the angled cross-guard. The blade met no resistance. He looked at Tafala, who still had an arrow nocked, then motioned with his eyes back into the aperture. She knew what he meant. Quickly she pulled back her bow and shot her arrow into the black. It clanked against a stone floor.

Rænon reached his arm inside the opening. His fingers followed the rock back a few inches until he felt a corner. Turning his hand, he grabbed the stone slab from the inside. He put his feet against the door's rock face. With all his strength he pulled outward, grunting. The top leftmost slab moved out slightly. He adjusted his grip on the slab from the inside and again pulled outward, this time planting his feet directly onto the bottom door slab as to stand up on it. His corded arms strained to move the rock segment. The stones ground together and again the slab moved outward, this time revealing its corner. Now he could wrench it aside and push it outwards to make a space large enough for him to fit through.

He jumped up on the lip of the slab and then disappeared into the dark.

Chapter V

Beyond the Tombdoor

The seven remaining members of the company emerged from the black mouth of the long, narrow tunnel through Albrunn. The flames of their torches cast a golden glow on the carved walls of the vast chamber in which they all now stood. By huge chains of ancient steel a cyclopean granite slab was suspended only a short length above the polished stone floor. The sides of the granite block were chiseled with more of the old Aelbrond speech. Along all four sides the runes stretched. *I am the sword of the Insane, rest for the formless, a guard in the war at the edge of the end.*

From their distance Rænon could see some of what lay on top of the perfectly hewn block. At least one thing was discernible—a giant skull.

Approaching slowly, more items upon the stone became visible. Laid out under the skull were the other bones, humanlike, but their proportions different. The skull was twenty times as large as a man's, and only at first glance appeared to have the features of a human. Each hand bore seven fingers, each terminating into long black points. A giant steel hammer lay below the left hand. Its face still gleamed ocher in the torchlight, as if the eons could not bring entropy upon it. The overlong jaws still held teeth, though they were sharp. The eye sockets were not like a man's, they were oversized pits of such deep blackness that their torches could not penetrate it. The skull was not wholesome to look at.

"This is our god, Farick?" said Rænon. "He doesn't look like the statues in Maehlin, the one I saw beneath the Iron Castle. Those looked like men. This is… it's…" He paused, unable to find the word.

"You're surprised that men made an image they were eased by?" asked Aarna, seemingly not taken back by the alienness of the dead god's anatomy.

"I shouldn't be." Rænon looked on Farick's bones solemnly. Between the arms and among the shattered rib cage sat a steel urn. Like the hammer, it was untouched by the corrosion of time. Around its gleaming circumference stretched more runes, dotted and jagged letters that Rænon strained to read. The company had all crept up onto the suspended granite block and brought their torches in to see for themselves.

This heart in steel
My ash in fire
A Godblade struck
In forge and pyre
Not Ill-Nitaar
Not Albrunn's spire
Will stand against
The Armor of Ire

Rænon read the runes aloud again. "These are the ashes of the mind and heart of Farick... I know what to do with them." Rænon looked at Aarna, who almost smiled.

Balan, unable to hide his disdain, spoke up. "Rænon, did you say The Armor of Ire? That's the creed of the Shattered Shields." Murk and Vaski eyed each other, each looking like he wished to clap Balan's mouth shut.

"It is," Rænon shot back quickly. "The Lourn Guards have never been able to get along with your brothers to the East, isn't that right?"

Balan stepped forward, to Murk and Vaski's visible discomfort. "They are not our brothers! They fight for Aelbrond but they might as well be Lanakians. Up there in the forest howling like wolves, they fight like beasts. They *are* beasts."

Rænon kept prodding. "They have never lost a battle, save for the battle of their namesake—"

"It's only a matter of time," Balan interrupted.

"Aye, and the Guards of Lourn would sing of it," Rænon said as he took a step forward as well.

Murk put his hand on Balan's shoulder to quiet him. "Rænon, pardon him, he only means that the Shattered Shields have made no effort to organize on the field. They are prone to primal tactics, ignoring defense, constantly attacking with such force that they rend everything, even their own."

Rænon was silent for a few moments, "If they die in battle it is a joy, if they win it is a joy. They cannot lose lest they be enslaved, and I cannot imagine that has happened even once. I admit I have admired them, and to boot, they hate the cult as much as I."

Murk spoke again, this time in a careful tone. "They saved us seven years ago in the sands of Navordi, but I will never forget what we saw that morning. The Shattered Shields came howling over the dunes. Some were naked, including the women. They fought with spiked chains and axes, swords that could only be swung with both arms. Not one of them carried a defense. We expected they would be free of shields, but they also wore no armor. Every Kynaran and Tarsulean that fell that day died in terror, piles of them. I have never seen such war-lust as I saw in the Vagarmen."

"Well, if Farick has anything to say about it, then the Shattered Shields may still have a part to play. Clearly there is war brewing again with Kynara and now Ill-Nitaar. And after I reforge this blade from these remains, we will be at war with a god itself, The Insane God," Rænon said stoically.

He picked up the urn, dropped the heavy steel lid and emptied it unceremoniously into his leather bag. The remnants of the mind and will of his god now weighed down on his right shoulder.

"Now that you have your quarry, how do we get out of here?" asked Tafala, who had clearly heard enough of the Aelbronders' bickering. "Are we to walk back through those tunnels and back down to Othra?"

Rænon took out the map again. The smeared blood of the Arhai cultist across the Arginese, made him think of Tavh and

Kedh. "From the map it looks as if we have walked all the way through Albrunn and down below the Plain of Othra. This tomb lies somewhere in the foundations of Albrunn. If we were able to tunnel through, we wouldn't have to dig far until we were beyond Othra and somewhere in the northern-facing Inner Ring, towards The Pit and Haiklan."

"Perhaps we can fit through this?" Kiv called out from the other side of the chamber, pointing her bow to a black opening in the carved-out granite wall. "I can hear water down there."

Rænon jumped down from the suspended block and moved towards her, Pitkeeper in hand. "I hear it, but the map has only one route, no other ways out from this chamber," he said as he lowered his head toward the opening. He could smell the river, which commingled the ferric odor of mountain water and the dank rot of a cave. "I'll climb in. Wait for my order to follow me, and this time I want you to listen."

The band could see Rænon's torch as he climbed down and landed on another floor that opened up into a room. "All right, climb in!" he yelled back up at them.

Once they were all standing on the floor their brands lit up the walls of the fanged cavern. This natural chamber was juxtaposed next to the hand-struck tomb at the end of old Aelbrond's journeying into The Shunned Mount.

It was a deep, though narrow and turbulent, river. It flowed in the direction they had been traveling through Albrunn, which was exactly what Rænon secretly hoped for. It exited the cavern through an eroded tunnel with high ceilings. Against the cavern wall near the mouth of the tunnel, something caught the Aelbronder's eye. "You see that?"

"A boat!" Kiv shouted.

It wasn't a large vessel. Had everyone in the band made it this far, they wouldn't all have fit. This struck Rænon as strange.

"Rænon, there is no telling where this goes," Aarna said gravely. "It could turn a corner and the ceiling could disappear as soon as we're too far to turn back."

"You're right. But why the boat? And in The Shunned Mount? Would the ancient Aelbronders fool us in this way? Besides, turning back and going down through Othra again is a poor option. I don't want to lose any more of you to the plain, forever riding around on the foul hornets of The Pit. I don't want that for myself."

"Aye!" exclaimed Vaski.

"Ah, good, another lover of liberty! Now, who wants to go back the way we came?" The band was silent. "All right, then let's test this vessel before our hopes are up," Rænon said. He tugged the ornately carved prow into river, keeping a tight hold on it so it wouldn't float away. "A steel craft, could be thousands of years old," he said while looking at Balan, who was staying quiet. He seemed deep in thought.

The band stood at the unlighted bank of the course. The Guards were preparing for the excursion by stripping off their heavier steel plates. The archers undressed even further.

"Will this work?" Tafala asked Rænon worriedly.

"I can only give you a dishonest answer. Do you want one?" he replied.

"No," she said as she casually shed her fur top and unburdened herself of the chain mail skirt she wore beneath. Her pale skin shone bright against the dark of the cave.

While most of the eyes were on the archers, Rænon emptied his can of torch oil onto his brand. Then he stealthily dipped it into his leather bag, filling it with the remains of Farick. He replaced the can back on his belt and walked over to Aarna, "Don't worry friend, I'll keep her afloat. Take this bag with the remains from the urn and keep it safe. I will have my hands full steering at the back of the boat." He could feel Balan's eyes on his back as he handed Aarna the bag.

"And what should we do with no oars, fold our arms and pray to Ylar's tits we make it?" Murk said jovially.

"Use your axes," Rænon shot back without humor. "Aarna, take the bow of the boat. Here's a piece of timber; use it as best you can. Kiv, Tafala, take care of each other behind Aarna and keep your torches dry. You three, in the back with me." Rænon pointed to the Guards of Lourn and motioned them to board as he took up the one main oar at the stern. It was made of a light, thin steel, like the boat. Balan seated himself right in front of Rænon.

The river moved swiftly. Rænon couldn't touch the bottom with the oar no matter how close to the bank he steered the craft. The ceiling remained high above the boat though from time to time the calcified talons of the cavern would reach down and the riders would have to dodge them. But for an hour or so the course held north and stayed calm.

Then came the sound that Rænon knew at some point he would hear.

"Rænon, you hear that?" Aarna called from the bow.

"Aye. You three, ready your axes, swift water ahead," he shouted.

Within seconds they were rushing past large, sharp rocks rising out of the surface of the swirling water. Along with the tapered formations on the ceiling, the rocks gave the tunnel the appearance of jaws filled with teeth, closing on the company.

The ceiling became shorter and the walls started to close in. The river's flow increased to an even greater speed. The Guards were trying to brake the craft by holding their axes flat against the strong current, but it did no good. They continued apace with Rænon steering the vessel through the jutting boulders. Aarna at the bow was using the ancient timber to steer and help Rænon as best he could through the course. The archers were balancing in the middle of the boat, attempting to keep their way lit and the torches dry.

Suddenly, a shaft of light from above pierced the darkness. Rænon looked up. For a moment they passed beneath a small aperture. He caught a glimpse of sunlight and sky, and then immediately they were again shrouded in darkness and torchlight. Keeping his eye on the jutting rocks he hoped there would be another break of light. This had to mean they were close to the Inner Ring.

"Looks like our brave leader was right, we might see ourselves at the end of this journey yet," said Balan in his now customary insolent tone.

"It strikes me, Balan, that you learned nothing from the guild, no respect from your commanders at Lourn," said Rænon. "If I get us out of here, King Hyrk will make you a rich man upon our return, yet you seem miserable about it."

"I will take my coin and head south."

"Lourn is east, Balan. You'll go south where? To Brederav, Runefare?"

"I will cross the river." Balan spoke in so hushed a voice that the rushing water covered his words.

"You'll what?"

"Rænon! More light ahead!" Aarna called from the front of the boat. Another shaft of light broke through the ceiling.

The river was taking gradual turns now and Rænon was losing faith that they still held a northern bearing. It seemed at the rate they had been traveling they must be somewhere in the bowels of the Inner Ring. The water was now foaming around the protruding rocks and the vessel was hitting more of them than it could dodge. Rænon tried to keep his focus on the river but he was still wondering about Balan's murmured plans.

Murk and Vaski paddled fiercely with their axes, pushing

off rocks that approached and sending sparks as blade and stone met. Balan was making a half-hearted attempt at the same task.

Another shaft of light from above.

The river was now moving at such a pace that the main oar at the back could do nothing to steer the craft. It was functioning as a rudder rather than an oar. Rænon held it tight against the clanging of submerged boulders. It jerked at his corded arms but he held it stable and still managed to remain balanced in the middle of the boat.

More light.

These were crevasses above them rather than small holes which let in sunlight as before. Now their way was lit more from the cracks of sunlight than the torches which the archers still held firmly. *We must be close,* Rænon thought to himself.

The river was seething. In the distance the sun broke through in front of them. "Rænon, we are almost out!" Aarna called back as the end of the cavernous course was in sight. But they seemed to be approaching too fast. The submerged boulders were now ramming into the bottom of the craft, rocking the vessel. The riders were lifted inches out of the boat and then landed hard. The water was white with rage. The Guards in back were struggling to make a difference with their axes to paddle through the course.

Another clash with a stone below the surface. Both archers flew forward. They let go their torches and braced their fall into Aarna, who in turn also fell forward and almost out of the boat. They were speeding to the mouth now but there were more frequent clusters of sharp granite protruding out in the short distance in front of them.

"Rænon, I think you misheard me earlier," Balan shouted behind him over the sound of white water.

"I think I must have," Rænon said loudly back.

"I will cross the river into Kynara, for you are on a fool's errand, and I must stop you."

Rænon, incensed, reached behind him to pull Pitkeeper from his back scabbard but Balan had been playing his move over in his head since they boarded the craft. He was quick to swing his axe while Rænon had his hand on the hilt behind his head. The axe bit into Rænon's side. He let go of the hilt behind him and grabbed the haft of Balan's axe while its blade was still embedded in his side.

"Snake!" Rænon yelled as the company turned around.

"Balan! Not now!" Murk shouted.

Blood flowed out onto the axeblade. Balan withdrew his weapon. Rænon went for the knife on his belt, but already Balan had cocked his axe behind him. He quickly thrust it forward, smashing Rænon in the face with the top of the axe.

Rænon's vision went white, then red, then he felt the cool water surround him. He hit the bottom of the river and was being swept along the current, bashing into the submerged boulders until, all of a sudden, he was held in place pinned between two large rocks. His scabbard was wedged in a way that held him in place, unable to grab the boulders right behind him on either side.

He heard the underwater grating of the scabbard against the rocks. He slipped in and out of consciousness but instinctually he resisted from taking a breath. One more moment, one more... The sound of his scabbard grating again. This time he felt himself become a bit free of the wrenched position he was in. With his last bit of strength he twisted his body, turned under the current and freed himself from the two submerged boulders.

His head shot out of the water. His first breath burned. The blood poured from his mouth and nose and forehead into his eyes. He held the wound in his side, trying in vain to stop the bleeding. He shouted a curse through broken teeth. The river had no mercy for him. Rænon bashed into rock after rock. He tried to take the hits on his unwounded side but would often hit his head or back. He lost sight of the boat, but he thought he could hear screaming. Again he faded out of consciousness, another rock, more black. He took a shallow breath, more black, more screaming, more black...

Chapter VI

Another Form

D*ryt unh meqmat, dryt unh! Axa Brakur!*

She stood among the ruins of the Iron Castle with the crisp air of the Arginese coming up the black cliffs and stinging her bare skin. The sun shone on the lush green of Isahin, the tumbling hills, the beautiful black stones, the writhing Insane God.

Narila repeated the words again, at the top of her breath, *"Dryt unh meqmat, dryt unh! Axa Brakur!"* Three of the demonic Starless Night sprinted through the castle ruins, past the short length of grass and off the cliff, plummeting into the Arginese.

Brakur convulsed, its massive form still a gruesome amalgamation of every corner of Hell. But it was no longer the size of the castle itself. Brakur was shrinking, changing form with every demon sacrifice and ancient phrase of Ill-Nitaar that Narila invoked. Now the writhing god would fit into the hall under the castle.

Again, more demons broke the circle and sprinted off the sheer black cliffs into the sea. The Insane God screamed, creating awful sounds that changed as its form did, each more horrifying and tortured than the last.

No longer the chimera that rose from the sea, Brakur flashed between anatomies wrought in the cold recesses of the cosmos, beyond the farthest stars and imaginings of the terrestrial underlords.

At times the form consisted of a gaseous mass, yet glistening as if wet, and also at once becoming rigid, spiked, full of eyes, then none at all. An open giant maw, a face only of fangs that dripped the nightmare bile of rotting planets.

Narila stood atop a broken column. Her large breasts heaved as she took in the cold sea air and yelled the words again, *"Dryt unh meqmat, dryt unh! Axa Brakur!"* The last of the Starless Night, a dozen or more, charged off the cliff.

Brakur shrunk, he became a man, then a child, then a woman like Narila but more beautiful. This was the form that troubled her most.

Brakur screamed again. The flesh turned dark, as dark as the Pit. The features faded into a black void lit by dim stars. The outline changed and no longer appeared human. Again it was formless and contained only one feature, the swirling unlit entropy acting rapidly on the universe.

"Eternity has broken you, Lord. You are lost in madness, an inescapable dream. And this, also appears like a dream to you... No! Those are your worshippers, down there in the waves, for you!"

Brakur slowly began to cease the rapid change and the form became stable. She could see now the outline of a head, a giant wyrm topped with shards of black that cut against the clear blue Isahin sky. Below the spiked crest there were no features of a face but only two eyes of white fire burning against a backdrop of dead cosmos. The wings spread like cloaks of black night sky. It lowered its head to Narila.

Chapter VII

Outside the Ring

Rænon hit the surface flat on his back. What little air that was in his lungs was knocked out. He felt as if the next breath were impossible. His head broke the surface and he gasped what air he could. The blood streamed down his forehead and into his eyes. He made a last dying effort to reach the shore only a few feet away. Again he fell into the void.

His eyes opened after minutes, or hours, no telling. Sand filled his right eye as his face was embedded in the bank. He chucked water, he tried to gain his breath, then wretched water again. He held his right eye closed and dug his fingers into the riverbank. Beneath the sand he felt knobby tree roots. He held them tight as he tried to replace the water in his lungs with air.

After gaining his breath he turned his head behind him. The sheer wall of the Inner Ring towered above, with a waterfall that started its descent at such a height he was unable to see it from his vantage directly below. *How could I have fallen so far?*

The falls terminated in a small lake. There were smoke pines clustered around the banks. Their grayish needles were distinct to the northwest corner of Aelbrond, near En-Faln and The Pit.

He was weak, feeling as if half his blood had left him. He tried to sit up but the long wound in his side burned. He yelled a curse across the lake that echoed over the waters. He spit blood onto the sand. Running his hands over his face, he discovered his front two teeth were missing and his nose was broken. *I'll gut Balan. How did I not see that coming?*

Then he remembered. His hand shot down to his belt. He grabbed the torch oil can and lifted the lid. It was full and dry. He felt as if Farick's gruesome face smiled upon his wretched form there, bleeding on the bank of the clear lake. Again a shock of remembrance. "Aarna!" he yelled. "Kiv… Tafala!" The names echoed as they bounced across the water and up the Inner Ring. There was no response but the sound of the cascading falls.

He lay there for a few moments, lost in visions of revenge. Then, holding his side, he labored to stand. His axe was gone. His dagger, though, was still secure on his belt, and Pitkeeper clung like his soul to his back. He grabbed the hilt behind him and pulled the sword to lean on like a crutch as he rose.

He walked along the water. No sign of the archers, no sign of his new enemies.

The bank was thick with pines. He kept close to it, looking for any evidence of the company or the boat. Then he saw something among the knees of a pine that reached far out into the water. Aarna was held there, tangled in the roots, his back pierced with more than a dozen treacheries.

"Aarna!" he yelled futilely as he saw the blue color of the old warrior's skin. "Cowards!" he yelled across the lake. He drew his sword, looking for any sign of Balan or the others. He jumped into the water, swam to his friend and turned him over. Aarna's face was creased from being submerged. *I must have been out for hours,* Rænon thought. "Balan! I'll find you!" Rænon shouted, holding his friend in the water.

It was clear to him from the landscape that he was in the northwest, just outside the Inner Ring. *I must be near Garucu. I'll get a horse there and ride to Maehlin, maybe I can catch up to Balan.* He lay Aarna back up on the bank and gathered stones around him. Rænon took a lock of his hair for the pyre-forge, along with his dagger, of which he was always proud. "You have no kin, but I will make a blade for our enemies, my friend. Sleep well."

Rænon was still weak. He rose slowly from the makeshift grave. He noticed the sun's position and limped off slowly west, towards Maydon Bay and the small village of Garucu.

Chapter VIII

Awakened Again and Again

Rænon stumbled through the open gates of the small village of Garucu. He had drained his flask during the trek from the lake, for it was his only source of pain-ease. Now he was drunk and bleeding, smiling at the concerned villagers through his missing front teeth. A woman gathered her children close to her as he passed by. An elderly man gave him a worried look but said nothing.

"Can we do something for you?" a voice called from behind Rænon. He turned to look.

A warrior clad in bear-fur, according to Aelbrond custom, stood there. He held a spear but was not aggressive towards Rænon; he was obviously concerned.

"I need a horse," Rænon said evenly.

"We have none for sale. You look like you need a healer before you need a horse," the warrior said. He was shocked that his fellow Aelbronder could even walk after suffering such grievous injuries.

Rænon reached onto his belt, pulled the knife that King Hyrk gave him from its sheath, and held it out for the warrior to see the touch mark on the blade.

"Guard Command!" The warrior stood suddenly straight. He

no longer gawked at Rænon's cuts but looked into his grey eyes. He slammed the shaft of his spear on the ground in attention.

"It's all right, no need for formalities. I need to get back to Maehlin. Do you have a horse or not?"

"You can have mine, commander!"

"I will never get used to that title. Thank you, I will make sure it is returned."

"It is yours, commander. May I ask who has done this to you? Where have you come from?"

"Three Guards of Lourn have forgotten their oaths. I've come from Albrunn."

The warrior's eyes went wide. "The Shunned Mount! No one has emerged from that place in a thousand years! And no one has passed through here in a few days… you say we should be looking for three Lourn Guards on the run?"

"Yes, his name is Balan, he has two cowards with him. If you can kill them, do so. Bring their heads to Maehlin and you will be a rich man. If you bring them alive you will be given a keep. Also, there are two archers from Haiklan who are our allies. If they are alive, give them whatever they need and tell them I have ridden to Maehlin."

"Yes, commander." The warrior tapped his spear on the ground again and ran quickly to the stables, returning shortly with a beautiful black and white mare.

"Her name is Haryndi, fastest horse in Garucu. Here, take

this water and saltmeat. You need it."

Rænon accepted the horn of water and bag of meat graciously. He took the reins from the warrior. "What is your name, friend?"

"I am Ficov, commander."

"I will make sure you are rewarded. Hooough!" And with Rænon's kick Haryndi took off out of the gates and southeast on the road to Maehlin.

He rode through the rest of the day and all through the night, pushing Haryndi as hard as he could. She slowed in the morning but he was already within sight of Maehlin's giant iron wall and the sharp, tapered turrets built incrementally along it. He spied Hyrk's towering castle beyond them, with the range of the Inner Ring behind the city, dwarfing it all.

"Alert the King, Rænon approaches!" The guards on top of the wall sounded their horns. They could see him alone on the plain before the gates. Rænon could barely hold tight the reins. His head slumped down and his back arched in the saddle. He swayed with the labored steps of Haryndi as she bore him towards the wall. By the time Rænon reached the iron gates and they creaked open, Hyrk had already rushed down from his throne to greet him.

"Rænon! Gods, you're alive!" Hyrk was shocked at the state of the Aelbronder. Dried blood matted his hair, stained his forehead, ran down his busted nose and mouth to his chin. His eyes were glazed over and Hyrk could tell by his color that he was short on blood. There was a leather strap around Rænon's torso keeping a bloody piece of torn fabric over the wound in his side.

He looked down at the king with vengeful grey eyes. "King, I chose the wrong company," he said before falling towards Hyrk's men, unconscious.

The ocherous light of torches lit the riveted timber walls. Rænon's eyes opened slowly. His vision was blurry, but a pair of Lourn Guards standing by the large door came into focus.

He leapt up and reached for his sword that he found leaning against the bed. He stood there naked, his free hand clenched.

"Rænon! It's all right, these men are mine," Hyrk said, sitting in a chair behind him on his other side. Rænon relaxed and lay back down on the bed. Beside Hyrk sat Kiv. She was dressed in a translucent robe through which he could see the marks of a fight on her pale skin. She had been slashed on the cheek and her ribs and right breast were dark with bruises.

"I can't believe you're alive," she said with wide eyes. "I'm sorry I left you behind but I waited at the falls. I never saw you emerge from the river or go over the edge. I was sure you were dead."

Rænon struggled to pull the memories out from the fog. His hand went to his side and discovered it had been stitched shut and a strong-smelling salve had been applied. More surprisingly, he felt teeth in his mouth again.

"Ah yes. We took the opportunity while you were unconscious to replace those for you." The king smiled at Rænon and handed him a mirror. Rænon grinned as two shiny metal teeth were fixed into his upper jaw. "Irontooth!" the big king laughed through his long grey beard.

"Not bad, these will do." He went on, "I remember feeling caught between the rocks in the cavern before I fell into a void. I don't know how long I stayed there but I awoke when the lake below slapped me back into life. I found Aarna there too, he was dead. You say you waited, where? And Tafala?"

"Balan took her," she said worryingly. "I waited on the ledge of the cliff after killing Vaski. The dumb bastard couldn't tie a proper knot to save his life—and it didn't."

Rænon sat straight up in bed. "Go on."

"After Balan attacked you in the boat, he cracked Tafala in the back of the skull. Then he ordered Vaski to grab me, which he did. Balan set upon Aarna, holding him down for Murk to stab him in the back. Then Balan tipped the boat deliberately and threw us all into the river only a few lengths from the falls. I won't forget watching Balan and Murk drag Tafala by her hair through the rapids and onto the ledge. Vaski was able to drag me up as well though we were on the opposite side of the river, on another ledge overlooking the falls. I let him hold me there. I waited for my moment. I could tell he was reluctant, they both seemed afraid of Balan."

"They'll die badly for this..." Rænon interrupted. "Forgive me, go on."

She began again, "We sat on opposite ledges. Balan tied Tafala's arms as she lay unconscious. He yelled over to Vaski to tie me as well and to climb down and meet them at the base of the Inner Ring. His exact words were that we would be a *worthy offering.*"

Rænon grasped the hilt of Pitkeeper tightly in his right hand. He was starting to understand the whole of Balan's intention.

Kiv went on, "Then I remembered you from our fight atop the Inner Ring… Vaski tied a rope around my neck and bound my arms behind me, but in his haste didn't realize it was too loose. As he turned me around, I stole the knife from his belt and shoved it up his jaw into his face. He screamed through the blade in his mouth. I kicked him off the ledge and I'll never forget how he screamed… all the way down. Balan and Murk couldn't retreat any faster down the rock face and out of my sight. They truly are cowards. I pity them."

"Pity won't save them," Rænon said in a low voice.

"I don't want it to," she said with a smile which quickly faded. "They still have Tafala. I climbed down the face of the Inner Ring, but the route took me down the northeastern direction. When I finally reached the ground, I was hours behind Balan. I ran southward around The Ring as fast as I could to catch up to them, but lost their tracks north of Garucu, so I came here to Maehlin to tell Hyrk of what happened. But I must go, *now.*"

Rænon looked to Hyrk gravely. "In what state are the Guards of Lourn? Is this the force we trust to defend Aelbrond?"

"Men are small, Rænon, oaths will be broken. Very few soldiers have dishonored the War Guild and lived into old age. We find them all."

"Well then, leave me to find Balan and Murk. And these men at the door, they now know everything, you say I can trust the—?"

Before Rænon could finish, the pair of Lourn Guards at the door drew their daggers. Each put the point to their own throats, drawing blood but keeping the knife still as the trickle ran down the blade and made big drops that hit the wooden floor loudly in the silence of the room.

"All right, men, no need for dramatics. I appreciate the gesture."

"I must find Tafala," Kiv said as she rose from her seat. "Wherever Balan can strike a deal with Kynara is where they are heading."

"Patience, Kiv," the king said as he motioned for her to sit again. "Rænon, have you forgotten why you went to the Shunned Mount?" Hyrk asked as he pulled from behind him the torch oil can.

"You found it! Want to know what it is?" Rænon asked him sarcastically.

"The contents of Farick's Urn?"

"It is."

Hyrk looked into the can with wide eyes. "The brain and bones of our underlord... Rænon, could you read the runes anywhere in the tomb? What did Farick look like?"

"Uncanny, Hyrk. Not like our statues, but he was our guardian and smith nonetheless. His hammer was there, I wish you could have seen it. I did read the runes and it seems we have a blade to make. King, if I still command the Guards of Lourn, gather our forces to cross the river Bruna. I advise we attack Kynara's largest army from the north. I will bring another force to assail the south and east. The west is up to you."

"I can send riders to Tarsul, but they are unpredictable and the cult of Arhai has an obvious presence there," the king said, tapping his foot on the floor planks. "Who do you have in mind to the south and east?"

"The Shattered Shields. I will take them with me to find Brakur, and others perhaps." The guards at the door eyed each other and Hyrk cracked a grin at Rænon.

Hyrk said, "That reminds me, I have one more surprise for you, Rænon. He comes all the way from Vyntane." The guards at the door unsheathed their swords and held them at the ready. One of them opened the door slowly.

From around the corner stepped a white, hairless and clawed foot, followed by the rest of the crooked form of a demon. This form Rænon recognized as one of the Starless Night. He grabbed Pitkeeper and jumped towards the demon. It recoiled, let out a shriek and fell backwards into the doorway again.

"Rænon, it's all right!" Hyrk shouted from behind him. "This one has turned against the cult!" Rænon's eyes burned as he held its red stare.

"How do you know? It speaks?" He held the point of his sword against the demon's neck.

"I speak! I speak!" cried the demon. "Barbarian, please... let me tell you what must be said." He put his clawed hand gently on the blade of the sword and pushed it away from his throat. Rænon still held it near, but far enough away to make him less nervous. "My name is Sedyt. I have come from Isahin, from under Vyntane, where the Insane God once wailed. You must... kill Brakur."

"But Brakur is your god, no? And how did you get here from Isahin, did you come by ship?"

"Noooo, I came *beneath* the sea. There are tunnels under everything, you know this... Brakur is my god, but he must die. The others like me, they are gone. When we die... we are pulled into his dream, into the eternal nightmare. I do not want to go. Some of the others did not want to go... but they did... now when Brakur wails, I can hear them too, screaming... please... end it."

"And what happens if I kill Brakur?"

"Nothing changes. Arginor, the world, it is his... it will rot... as it would have."

Rænon held his blade still but lowered his head and stared for a moment at the floor. "I am in no mood to trust a man, even less a demon."

"The consequence of not taking my word... is too much... eternity claims the sanity of everyone, even gods. If you die while Brakur is in our realm, you will be pulled in."

Kiv still stood at Hyrk's side; they both wore grave faces.

Rænon returned their look. Sedyt went on, "Brakur, and the one who can… speak to him, a woman, they have gone to Nitaar. She wants to keep him there forever, to protect the way to eternity. You must go there."

"Hyrk, where are we?" Rænon said flatly.

"We're near my castle, in the house of my healer, Daxu. You've been out for two days."

"We must go to the pyre-smithy. Then I will need a ship."

Chapter IX

Ill-Nitaar

"The obsidian coast!" the spotter called from atop his perch on the Kynaran vessel. "Balan, we should land before sundown," he shouted down again.

After a few minutes Balan could see the sharp spires of jet stabbing out of the sea like a protective battlement against all comers. They rose up into the dimming sky, impaling the sun on the horizon. He looked over the deck to the main mast where Tafala was chained. Already she was staring at him with hateful eyes.

Murk stood beside Balan on the deck. "What in the hell have I done, Balan?" Murk said, also looking with dread upon the ominous coast of the Ill-lands. "Vile Nitaar, that's where this has brought us, my fellow guard. You acted in haste killing Rænon, now we fight for Kynara and the Cult of Arhai. I am sickened by myself."

"Don't be afraid, my friend, we are on the winning side. Rænon would have made the Godblade and brought down the Shattered Shields, of all armies, to fight Kynara on their own soil. Trust me, we are better off behind the lines than on the field of that battle." Balan spoke in a tone too sanguine for the circumstances, Murk thought.

As they drew closer to the acicular coast, they could see a break in the skyward-reaching angular formations. An immense black rectangle formed a long straight line until the thin, sharp rock formations began again.

A strange sound rang out, high pitched at first, then forbiddingly low, then up again to a pitch that nettled their ears.

"Gods, Balan."

"Get a hold of yourself, Murk. Do not show weakness here. We've come to bargain."

The black rectangle began to rise into the sky. Slowly, the crew of Kynarans began to whisper dark phrases of supplication. The arrant block seemed to be a gate leading into a canal, but it rose without hinges, no machinery. It simply hung in the air above the water, high enough for the largest ship in Arginor to pass under.

"You two have no idea what you've done by coming here," Tafala said as she stared up at the black gate floating over them. "You would've been better off running into the northern waste than coming here to strike a bargain with these fanatics."

"You were either on the side of a god or the side of a sword," Balan replied quietly.

"I would choose a sword over a god that went insane, you twit," she fired back.

"Well, Rænon is dead, the ashes are gone, and there is no sword, so get comfortable." Balan walked over to her and tightened the chain which held her arms around the mast behind her back. He moved around to the front of the archer, standing close to her so as to push her large bosom against his chest. While staring into her baleful eyes, he said, "Stay quiet. These Nitaarians can make your death quick or very long."

The ship entered the canal and the floating gate descended behind them with no sound. They were now inside the Ill-lands. All of the barren features from the coast persisted deeper into the territory. There were no trees, no vegetation, only the uncanny landscape of dark blasted rock with a cape of black mountains on the far horizon and dense, hoary clouds hanging above them.

The same noise that rang out before the gate rose in the air sounded out again, this time much louder, shriller. Now the passengers of the Kynaran vessel could see dark shapes running between the obsidian formations. Shrouded heads would peer over the top of a jagged boulder and then shoot down again. The sound rang out once more, a high-pitched note which dropped obscenely low and then back up again to a stinging register. Some of the Kynarans held their ears, while others dropped to their knees on the deck, offering prayers in the Ill-speech of Nitaar.

Both Balan and Murk stood silent and still with their hands on the hilts of their swords. Murk looked to Tafala who had her head down, murmuring something to herself.

The sheer walls of the canal were equal in height to the top of the vessel's highest sail, but it was still unclear where the canal would end and where the dark waters were bearing them. There was no turning around in this narrow, fast-moving channel.

"Ah, finally! You must sail as slowly as Brakur flies!" A sultry voice shouted down at the ship from atop the channel wall. The crew looked up to their right-hand side. Pale skinned men clad in black tunics threw looped ropes which caught the demon's head prow of the Kynaran vessel. Another rope was thrown out, catching the stern columns at the aft. The vessel was now held in place by the shore.

"My fellow Kynarans, and your company of deserters, I am Narila." She stepped forward to the edge of the canal wall, between two carved obsidian statues of some night-bound creatures of Nitaar. She wore nothing other than a thin blue robe which she didn't bother to tie at the waist. Her nearly naked figure stood with both hands on her hips in defiance of the chill wind. With eyes of different colors she looked down at the vessel and surveyed the crew.

"You two Aelbronders, I understand you have left the Guards of Lourn?"

"Yes, Narila, with no trepidation," Balan shouted up at her. "When Brakur was summoned the world was divided between those faithful and those who would rather die. We have faith."

"Faith! What do you need faith for? Brakur is here, on his creation with his acolytes, the Arhai. These men do not want faith, they want to defeat death! You godless Aelbronders will never understand."

"I understand wholly, and if you can secure for me eternity then I offer you the death of the one who sought to stop you, one named Rænon. And here, we have also brought you a gift, as we heard in Navordi you have been afflicted with boredom. This should stave it off for a while." He drew a knife from his boot and walked over to Tafala. He cut the shirt off the girl. Her massive breasts, now on display to all, heaved as she anxiously took rapid breaths.

"Now I'm starting to like you, Aelbronder," Narila said as she admired the semi-nude form chained to the mast. "So you have killed Rænon? Well, that is something. I sent a company of Kynarans loyal to Arhai with a *special three* to kill him. It seems you have done what they could not."

"Yes, we fought them on The Inner Ring. This one killed your demon-priest!" He poked at Tafala's shoulder.

"Oh, well, she will pay a price for that!" Narila caressed her own belly. Her hand went down between her legs for a moment before she suddenly stopped herself.

"Allow us to fight for you, fight for the Arhai!" Balan shouted up to her.

"We will see. Pull them in!" She shouted orders to the Nitaarians tending the ropes which held them in port. They quickly untied the ropes from their obsidian anchors atop the wall. Scores of them started to pull the vessel toward the carved-out dock onto which the Kynaran ship could disembark.

The small band of Kynarans in their crimson-colored armor of boiled leather marched along the path through the barren expanse of sharp rock. Thirty or so hearty men, all sworn to the

Cult of Arhai, followed a band of Adyrtun warriors brandishing black stone axes, none of whom would touch steel. Balan and Murk followed in the back of the line with Narila who led Tafala by a chain around her neck. She yanked it cruelly when the exhausted archer lagged behind.

"I must thank you Balan, and you—what was your name again?"

"Murk," he said, not quite meeting her eyes.

"Murk, yes, you are a quiet one. And what did you do as Balan killed Rænon?" Narila questioned.

"I killed his friend," he said solemnly.

"Oh, the pangs of guilt," she said, sensing his regret. "I have heard of them."

Balan tried to divert her attention away from Murk. "How do you know so much about events so far away?" he asked.

"I learned the Ill-speech as a child, before going to Isahin. After I survived the fall of Vyntane and Rænon's attempt to kill me… I pleaded to Brakur to make me whole again. Now I have the grey eye of an easterner, but he did his best. With the right words I can wake him for a time. He thinks I am a good dream so he seeks me, follows me through rolling nightmares. He tells me what I ask him of the world when I can get him to see me. Otherwise he thrashes about in many forms, which is not good to watch."

Balan thought for a moment. "Listen, there are other pieces of Farick that remain in the Shunned Mount. Another man might seek to make the Godblade and use it against Brakur. I assume that's what Brakur wants, that's why he created Farick in the first place, as a guard."

"Brakur must not die, no matter what he wants. If he dies we lose everything. Soon we will invade Aelbrond. Balan," she said with an uncertain tone, "if you have killed Rænon, you have bought us all the time we need to gather our forces in Kynara. I have sent riders all over Arginor. I've garnered favor in Tarsul, and even King Hardboar in Haiklan, without Hyrk's knowledge of course, has sworn to Arhai. Aelbrond and the godless savages in the east will be overcome. And after all enemies of the cult are crushed, I will tear down Shunned Albrunn and blow its dust into The Pit."

"And what of The Western Isles?" Murk said, ruining her moment.

"I spotted some of their ships patrolling the coast of Isahin before I came here to Nitaar. I assume they will stay loyal to Aelbrond, so they can die as well."

Balan felt assured by her words. Murk stayed silent. "I couldn't help but notice you said Brakur *flew,*" said Balan. "How did you get to Nitaar from Vyntane?"

"On his back," she said. "Now shut up, we are here." After cresting the summit of the small hill they were climbing they looked down into an immense valley. In the vale was a sprawling city with soaring stone towers of a seemingly impossible architecture. "Welcome to Shar-Kut," Narila said, holding Tafala's chain tight.

As they trekked down the slope more features of the city became distinct. Bulbous towers rose tall and strange. They were hewn symmetrically and gave the impression of falling droplets of water. They had round, wide bases that tapered upwards to invisible thinness, yet they could support the weight of many more droplet-shaped rooms above it, all connected by their own thin beam. At the topmost room the tapered point stretched skyward into a long, thin black needle, making the city appear like a bed of spikes. There were small windows in the round rooms with carved embellishments around them. Golden light shone out of a few, but many more were unlit. There were other buildings, also made of stone, but the stone used was of a lighter shade than the black landscape they had just traversed. These also had a round, organic quality, being either wholly circular or semi-circular in design.

There were also many large burrows in the ground, black tunnels that had carved masonry around their mouths, ringed with strange runes of the Ill-speech.

In the center was the citadel, taking the bulbous qualities of the lesser towers into the absurd. Giant round fortifications that stood on singular thin vertical foundations were connected by what seemed to be dark translucent glass. There were hundreds of such sections connected to the others, reaching up into the sky. The construction could not be accounted for by Tafala or the traitors from Aelbrond. They stared at the vista in disbelief.

In front of this impossible fortress was a great rectangular fountain filled with inky water. Columns of azure and emerald rose up around its edge and supported another frame that spilled dark water into the pool below. The top frame was made of stone, but it must have been hewn by some unknown method. It dipped and looped and was embellished in great detail to appear like some profane eel pulled from the depths.

In between the columns were carven statues. Every manner of blasphemous creation imaginable was represented. From their mouths, or eyes, or claws, black water spilled forth into the pool.

The company crossed the threshold of Shar-kut's defensive wall and walked straight toward the citadel. The path lead through a cobbled street flanked with teardrop towers. They came to a stop next to the great fountain with its cyclopean idols. Standing next to the massive sculptures, the company looked like insects in comparison. Tafala gazed upon the idols with dread, then she looked over to Murk. He refused to look at it, keeping his stare straight on towards the strange castle. She could see his hands were shaking.

Balan looked up at the skybound citadel. "Is this Unvon's keep?" he asked Narila.

"It is."

"Who is Unvon?" Tafala questioned.

"He is the High Priest of the Arhai and ruler of Nitaar. He asked that you all be brought to his court when you arrive. Now you, close your trap. You two, follow me but say nothing unless you are asked."

Balan couldn't resist. "Have I not earned a word with the king?"

"Your treachery was invaluable to the cult, and I do appreciate you bringing me a plaything." She tugged at Tafala's chain. "The Kynarans I sent to Albrunn were disposable but the other three were sent by Unvon himself. The demon-priest was his friend. And you must know how much Nitaarians hate you Aelbronders. Keep your mouth shut and you will survive."

Narila jerked the chain, making Tafala catch herself with a long stride, and led Balan with Murk close behind. They passed the thirty or so Kynarans sent to fortify Shar-kut and offer protection for Brakur. Then they passed the bleached-skinned Adyrtun soldiers that hissed at them through sharp teeth and stared hatefully with cerise eyes. Up a great staircase and over an even greater landing stood another thousand or so Nitaarian soldiers, arrayed in lines and holding their obsidian axes in front of their chests in a ready position. A path was cut through them straight to a large open portal in the keep's center.

The immense circular stone door floated above it in the same manner that the seagate rose when they entered the canal. There were no hinges, no man-made engineering held it aloft. It was big enough that should it fall, it would crush them and hundreds of soldiers. They walked quickly under the floating slab and through the portal to another wonder of alien architecture. This was a giant room with perfectly hewn columns of azure and deep green, like the fountain outside but even taller, which held up an arched ceiling hundreds of feet above. In the center of the room there was a great obsidian pyramid with carved steps leading to a throne that was hewn out of the cyclopean rock as well. The back of the throne rose up and tapered to a sharp pinnacle high above the smooth marble floor. Leading the way to the throne were another thousand or so Nitaarian spearmen standing at attention, flanking a long inlayed obsidian path that terminated at the steps of the giant black pyramid.

Suddenly the strange hall rang out with an awful scream, the scream of a thousand men, a thousand demons at once. It was so loud and tortured that even some of the Adyrtun soldiers dropped their heads and winced.

"Damn you, Balan," Murk whispered.

They continued to walk towards the giant throne. Unvon sat upright upon it, bent forward to squint at the quartet.

"Ah, Narila! And what have you brought from Kynara? Are these Aelbronders? And a woman?"

Even from the floor his bright yellow and red eyes were visible to them. His face was chalk white and his lips were stained and dark. He was hairless, without brows or beard. He had the features of a man-thing living in sunless caves for thousands of years. Upon his head was an obsidian crown ringed with tall, thin spikes, each at least a foot high. Otherwise he was clad much like his soldiers: he wore obsidian plated armor, two pieces that covered his broad chest connected by eel leather straps to shoulder plates that were sharpened and pointed. He wore no shirt over his black-veined, sinewy torso. On his forearms were faceted polished gauntlets of the same black stone of which the pyramid was constructed. Long black claws protruded from his hands and his bare feet. The claws clicked on the smooth throne as he surveyed the foreigners.

Narila stepped in front of Tafala to answer. "Yes, Unvon, these two men have killed our most dangerous enemy, Rænon, the one who would forge the Godblade and bring it against us."

"Ahhhh, Raaaaaaanon," Unvon groaned the name. "Yes, killer of many of our men and allies. You two now swear to Arhai?" Unvon looked on the two former Guards of Lourn skeptically.

"Yes, my king," pronounced Balan.

"Yes, my... king," said Murk.

"And this one, who is she?" Unvon asked, pointing a black claw at Tafala.

"She is mine, my lord, a gift all the way from Haiklan," Narila said as she stepped away from Tafala, allowing Unvon a better look at her prize.

"Ahhhh yes, you like your games. You can have her, for a time. But eventually she will have to go to the fountain."

"Thank you, Lord Unvon."

Tafala raised her head at this. "The fountain? Like the one outside? Like hell!" she snarled at the king.

Unvon leaned over like a beast and ran down the steps headfirst on all fours. Within seconds he stood before Tafala, exhaling hot, putrid breath through black teeth into her face. For the first time in her life she felt close to fainting. Then her anger pulled her out of it. "I'm not afraid," she bluffed.

"Good, it will be more pleasant to watch you *become* afraid," Unvon said sardonically, still within an inch of her face.

"It is a wonder there are no women here. You are such a *fair* king." Tafala managed the sarcastic rejoinder, in spite of her quivering lips.

Unvon stood back a pace. Clearly this was the first time anyone had spoken to him this way. Narila yanked at her chain, bringing her down to her knees.

"Ahhh, yes, the women. They are gone," Unvon said with a smile that allowed a trickle of drool through the corner of his wide mouth.

"The city is only men?" Tafala said from her knees.

"There are a few women, the ones who will fight," Unvon offered.

"Where are the rest? The children?"

"They were sacrificed."

"Monster! Why!" Tafala shouted.

Narila slapped her in the mouth. The blow drew blood that dripped down her chin and onto her naked chest. "To bring Brakur here, where he is safe," she said scoldingly to Tafala.

"With you on its back," Tafala accused, struggling in her bonds.

"Someone had to hold the reins." Again Narila yanked the chain cruelly.

Unvon grabbed Tafala's face, digging his black claws into her cheek. He spoke sinisterly. "While Brakur is here we share in his existence, in his nature. If we can keep him here forever, we will live forever."

"So if I kill you, you will become part of a god's nightmare?" Tafala said, holding his stare.

"Not if the gods accept our *final* sacrifice, the offering to stay Brakur's mind. After we crush Aelbrond we will put the life of every living thing that does not swear to the Cult of Arhai to the flame, or to the fountain. I think I will feed you to the God of the Fountain myself."

"How many gods do you have?" Tafala was baiting him now, realizing she might be the only person in Arginor to hear the cult's plan.

"More than you, barbarian! Brakur had to be pulled out of his dreaming and brought back into his creation. The Starless Night accomplished that with their sacrifice. We offered our wives and children to the God of the Fountain and now Brakur was able to come here where he is safe. Now we will offer up every soul in Arginor as an offering to stay his mind."

"How do you know the sacrifice will work?" Tafala prodded.

"There is nothing greater we can offer, it must work. *Nishu ag Nitaar, felu tyn nat Arhai!*"

"Yes, yes, send your thousands..." spat Tafala. "These spearmen and those axemen outside won't last the day. I don't care how many Kynarans you command."

Unvon clenched his clawed fist and struck her jaw. She was knocked out, but his pride had taken a blow in front of his soldiers. He leaned in close to Narila. "I will allow you to take her down to your hall, but you must break this one for me, before I feed her to Yadu-sha in the fountain." He looked to the two Aelbronders. "And send these two to the front lines in Kynara with the rest of our force. They still must prove themselves loyal to Arhai. Besides, there is no use for them here."

"My lord," Balan beseeched, "if you—"

Unvon dug a claw into Balan's neck. "Beg me once more and I will let these men spear you and feed you to Yadu-sha on skewers." Balan was silent. Murk met his fearful eyes and gave him a scornful look.

Then, a thousand screams at once. Screams of men, of demons, of women and children rang out through the massive hall.

Unvon walked over to the Nitaarian commander that stood nearest to the throne's stairway. He was a pale giant, iron-thewed, with a face twisted from generations of Nitaarian inbreeding. "Brakur wails without end. Gather our forces to set sail at sunrise."

Chapter X

The Godblade

Rænon swung his hammer hard. He was in the process of forging the stock longer by using half-faced hammer blows on the edge of the anvil face, tapering the tip of the would-be blade. The anvil's ring carried off into the streets of Maehlin. The pyre-smithy had stood in the center of the city for millennia, open for anyone to come and make an ancestral blade with the remains of a loved one. This blade was to be no ancestral blade; this sword would contain the essence of a god, and as such, a part of Brakur itself.

The sword would be longer than Pitkeeper, more narrow and thinner. Rænon had taken the time to fold many layers of hardstruck steel together with tougher steel, striking hard when it glowed bright yellow and welding the layers together. Now that he had the blade forged to his preferred shape and length, it was time to harden and imbue it with the remains of Farick.

First the remains were poured in a ceramic urn and placed in the middle of the coal forge. Rænon worked the bellows of the forge for an hour, slowly turning the contents of the urn into charcoal. Once the charcoal was formed, he placed it in a mortar and ground it with the pestle until it was a fine powder. He then took salt from the Arginese Sea, a bit of *whetchar* from Duna and added it to the ground charcoal mixture. Next he added water, making the dry mixture formable, and encased the blade in it. Then he wrapped the encased blade in another layer, this one of clay. He placed it back in the forge, working the bellows so that the case glowed consistently gold and that it would pull the hardness out of the coal and into the blade. He watched it in the forge for over an hour, then took the blade out. He broke off the ceramic casing, then cracked the layer of charcoalized remains that had entered and changed the sword while in the heart of the forge. He placed the blade once more in the forge, waited for the glowing color he desired to see, and then plunged the blade into the old iron quench tank filled with black oil and Nitaarian blood. He pulled the sword out of the quench. It was on fire. He could hear a faint sound coming from the blade, the sound of screaming, a tortured yell. He ran a rasp over the blade, it skated across with a high pitched *shring.*

Hyrk was watching from the doorway. "The Godblade!" he exclaimed.

Rænon smiled. "Aye, the hardblade!" He tapped it on the anvil and it sung a high note. He put it up to his eye and stared down the blade, inspecting it. "And it stayed true! I will name it *Voidcaller.* Now to give it a temper, a handle and an edge. You care to help?"

Hyrk grinned. "Aye, I'm good as a striker, if you need one."

"A king to strike for me! I don't think I'll get that chance again." He handed Hyrk the big sledge.

They spent the evening forging the elements for the hilt and then affixed them to the blade, which had been tempering in a boiling bath of blood since midnight.

It was now first light and the sword was almost ready. Rænon sat at the grindstone, keening the edge while Hyrk admired the blade. It was almost four feet long. The shape of the blade was typical of an Aelbrond longsword, having a convex peak which ran down the center line of the blade all the way to the tapered point. The steel cross-guard angled upwards slightly and each end of the guard terminated into a faceted spike. The handle was wrapped in black leather and overlaid with gold filament. The pommel was forged into a spiked skull-cracker so that it could be deadly from both ends.

It was a big sword, but deceptively light as Rænon tested its edge on a piece of leather. It went through the piece as if he had swung it through the air. He then picked up an old metal helm that lay in the corner of the smithy. Voidcaller cut through not just the thin steel helm, but into the stump on which he had placed it as well. He had never seen a blade cut so well or so effortlessly. Next he tested it on a brass cuirass. Rænon almost fell forward as the blade bit and went through the breastplate like it was made of wax. "Ylar's tits, Hyrk, is this sorcery?"

"Hmmm, sorcery, an unknown natural law of the gods, who knows. This is what Farick always wanted to be, what he was fated to be. The sword will never need another edge. It will become even more trenchant on the bones of your foes."

"Hyrk, tell me, how did you learn so much?"

"I know nothing, Rænon. Being king is usually a boring affair, and so I read all day most days."

"But you seem to know of the gods, the lesser gods, the things that seem unknowable."

"I only know what the texts say, but I don't know if they are true."

"I see," Rænon replied. "Let's assume they are true since many strange things have occurred in the last few months—more than I have seen in my short life."

"The texts say that one day Brakur will come back to this realm, awakened from his aeon-long slumber for a short time. The Cult of Arhai will sacrifice much to bring Brakur to Nitaar where he can be protected, and so the Arhai can live forever, even after their death, sharing in his dreams."

"But the god is mad, living in some nightmare. It wants to be killed."

"The cult does not truly care about Brakur, they only want eternity. The texts tell of a great sacrifice of every enemy of the Arhai, one great enough to restore Brakur's mind for the sake of themselves."

"And who would this sacrifice appease?"

"No telling. They pray to all gods, except Farick of course. There are lesser gods in Nitaar, and they speak of other gods, outside the cosmos."

"Other gods?"

"There are worse things than Brakur. There are over-gods,

wrought with blind spots, ridden with paradox."

"And beyond them?"

"An over-law of nothing."

"And this is in the text of the Arhai?"

"No, this comes from the prose of Farick."

"I see," Rænon said again. "Can you see why I don't read these books?"

"I can! But you've read Farick's own handwriting. His home was Shunned Albruun before he was killed and sealed inside."

"The runes in the tomb were his?"

"Yes, he prepared his own tomb as he knew his fate. This is the reason for his existence, to show us the pyre-forge and give us his body for the blade. So that we would be ready."

"Ready for what?" Rænon asked skeptically.

"The war at the edge of the end."

Rænon looked down at his sword.

Chapter XI

Theatre of War

"It is true, I'm afraid. We spotted a fleet of Haiklan mareships bearing south along the coast of Tarsul. They flew the Banner of Arhai."

Lord Sanhar spoke gravely to King Hyrk. They stood in a circular room in Runefare's ancient stone tower system before a great granite table with a large map of Arginor painted on its surface. Surrounding the table were the kings and commanders of Aelbrond, Larion, The Red Jewel, and Lanak, along with Kiv and Rænon. Sedyt was there was well, the traitor to his own kind, the Starless Night. Now, due to his dark knowledge, he was a welcome member of this war council.

Sanhar continued. "All of our ships from Larion and The Jewel were already inside Maydon Bay when we spotted them. They either didn't see our ships or decided not to engage us. I think it was the latter." Sanhar looked around the room.

Hyrk shook his head. "In the dark corner of my mind I knew this. Of the band of riders I sent to Tarsul, only one returned this morning, and he had a grim tale. He reported the rest of my men were killed in Disna, put to the torch as an Arhai sacrifice, and riders from Tarsul went north to Lindoch, apparently to join Haiklan in this war against us." He took a large breath. "I see Haiklan has been persuaded. Cowards."

"That isn't all," Sanhar went on. "What brought us to rally our own fleets and sail here... days ago in the sky we saw something, and someone, flying over The Red Jewel and my keep. A crimson wyrm with long taloned wings, shining eyes of white fire. On it sat an unclad woman, raven haired, with a bosom you could see from the ground."

"That was Brakur, and Narila!" Sedyt exclaimed. "That is the form he would take. They were going to Nitaar." When Sedyt spoke he made the other men uneasy. He only loosely resembled a man. He had the crimson eyes, sharp teeth and savage aspect of a demon from the bowels of the earth. His voice hissed, it was raspy and at times guttural. But he hated the cult and wanted to see Aelbrond and its allies crush the Arhai, and that was enough for the men in the room.

"Narila!" Rænon exclaimed. "Is that the woman you said can speak to Brakur? She lives? I cannot believe it... though I should. Balan probably thinks I'm dead too."

"There was one more thing," said Sanhar. The other men from The Jewel and Larion put their heads down solemnly as their lord continued. "On our way to Runefare in the towns along Tarsul's northern coast we saw the burning embers of gruesome rites. Men had burned their families, towns had burned their men, heads sat on pikes, likely of those who would not kneel to the Arhai. The takeover of Tarsul is complete. Haiklan is likely much the same."

"They are glowing iron, these maniacs who would burn us to appease dark gods," said Rænon. "We must smash the cult on the anvil of Kynara, and I am the hammer that strikes. I say we sail out the bay and down the coast with the whole of Aelbrond's fleet." His fist was clenched on the granite map.

Utrok, wild ruler of Lanak, stood towering at least a foot over the rest of the men. He was quiet for much of the meeting, spending most of his time staring at Sedyt, but finally broke his silence. "I have brought a force of over two thousand riders. When we crossed into Aelbrond and passed through Dargoa we picked up the Shattered Shields, who have no leader, as you know, and they marched behind us. They are at least four hundred in number camped outside Runefare. My men are with the Guards of Lourn in the city's barrack hall." The giant Lanakian ruler looked to Hyrk as he spoke.

"Thank you, Utrok, this won't be forgotten," Hyrk said, taking Utrok's big hand and shaking it sincerely. He turned to the rest of the leaders. "I say we should take our ships to Sish. It is the closest city for Haiklan, Tarsul, and Nitaar to gather their forces together with Kynara. Also, the prose of Farick says the battle will be on *crimson shores.* That can only be Sish."

"I would take the Shattered Shields with me to Nitaar," Rænon said urgently. "The battle is near, a few days' time. I need to get to the Ill-lands and north again to Kynara as quickly as possible."

"Take them, before the Guards of Lourn and the Vagarmen kill each other," Utrok said with a rough smile.

"I am going with you," said Kiv immediately. "If Tafala is in Nitaar then I will be there. If she is in Kynara then I will be there too."

"Good, your bow is welcome, and you might be the only archer with us," said Rænon. "Hyrk, I think we should split the Guards of Lourn. Let us take the cavalry with Utrok's Lanakian riders and cross the Bruna into Kynara to assail Sish from the north. The rest of the Lourn Guards and Aelbrond's infantry can man our vessels along with the fleet from The Jewel and Larion."

"I agree, that's the best course," said Hyrk. "There are many Guards of Lourn who want to prove themselves to you after Balan and Murk's treachery. But are you sure that you will only take the Vagarmen? You may need an element of tact in the Ill-lands."

"I don't require tact on this mission. I need *the armor of ire."*

"Ah yes, I almost forgot, the runes," Hyrk said with reverence, straightening his back.

"I will take command of the Guards of Lourn once I meet you and the fleet after my return from Nitaar. How many Kynarans make up their main army?" asked Rænon.

"The last we heard, about a thousand on horseback, another six thousand in the infantry and another thousand from the east, some riding the talix."

"The talix? Bastards. All right, let's just say Haiklan, Tarsul and Nitaar add another twelve, so that we face the field against twenty thousand fighting men. How many do we have, all told?"

"With Larion, The Red Jewel, and Lanak's aid, we have almost ten thousand," Hyrk answered.

"Very good," Rænon said.

"Half is good?" Utrok questioned.

"It's not bad. It means we only have to kill two men each, and the Vagarmen won't be happy unless they kill twenty." Rænon cracked a smile that raised the spirits in the room.

Hyrk turned to Utrok. "Will you do me the honor of leading your men along with our Guard Cavalry to attack Sish?" he asked as he held the giant king's eyes.

"Aye, would be my honor, King Hyrk."

"We are in your debt, Utrok." the King of Aelbrond said while slightly bowing his head to him. "Rænon, I will take the Aelbrond fleet down the coast and wait offshore for you to return from Nitaar before we storm their shores." Lord Sanhar and the silent Lord Koldur from Larion nodded their heads in agreement.

"A sturdy plan," said Rænon. "I will leave now and I suggest the cavalry get moving. There won't be many fighting men in the towns in Kynara to give you any trouble, but avoid them if you can. My king, grant me the biggest vessel we have. I must lead these soldiers from only one ship, so it must carry all four hundred men."

"*Wavelord* is our greatest ship. Take her," Hyrk said with no hesitation. "And the ruler of Nitaar, Unvon, is also high priest of the Arhai. If you can kill or capture him, all that will remain is a headless army for us to bury. Follow a southwestern bearing and land as close as you can to Shar-kut. Their gate will be shut and the ship will be crushed against the obsidian shore if you tried by way of the canal. There is a strand to the west, you can land there."

"Thank you, king," said Rænon. He looked to Kiv, who was staring at the black isle of Nitaar on the map.

Sedyt spoke up, his croaking voice startling the others. "I would ride onto the field of battle on a great stallion… for I've never ridden. I would wield the greatest sword my arms can lift, for I have never once touched steel. It would do me a great honor to ride with you, Utrok, against the Arhai," Sedyt said, bowing his pale head to the giant Lanakian king.

Utrok paused before answering. "Get this demon a horse and let's ride."

Chapter XII

The Storm

W*avelord* cut through the white caps, driven fast southward by a sudden gale that whipped at the axen-banner of Aelbrond from the main mast. The red sun was rising on the starboard side after a full day and a half's journey towards the Ill-land. With the new light they could see an anvil-shaped cloud on the horizon, dark and foreboding. The wind at the galley's back drove them straight on toward the storm.

"Rænon, it's Nitaar!" yelled Kiv from her perch atop the mast.

Within moments he could see the black acicular coast himself, though it was miles away. The land on the starboard side seemed more even, lower in the horizon and lacking the sharp features of the obsidian coastline.

"We must have followed the star-bearing correctly, because we have hit our aim just west of the channel of Shar-kut," Rænon said as she climbed down.

The winds picked up rapidly as the flat top of the storm cloud dominated the horizon. A chill wind at their back from the northwest pushed them toward the rocky coast.

Rænon stood at the stern of the trireme galley where he helmed the vessel's two main oars. Below the deck three levels of oarsmen pulled ninety oars on each side of the vessel, with two Vagarmen manning each oar. The remaining Shattered Shields were serving as deckhands but at the moment stood idle, staring off the bow to the dark scene.

The piper played a steady, rhythmic tune that kept the oars in time and without foul as Rænon gave him directions from the helm. Hard they pushed against the developing wind from the west. The dark anvil in the sky began to crack with thunder. Lightning shot down onto the Ill-lands. The piper kept perfect time over the clamor of the storm. Rænon leaned hard into the main oar, trying to steer the giant craft in preparation for a possible landing, although the shore was still miles off.

The Shattered Shields have an undue reputation, Rænon thought as he admired the synchronicity of the oars. They were quite organized when they needed to be. They were rough, square-jawed and dark-eyed hardmen from the northeast. Most were just above six feet and were broad of shoulder. Many were unshaven and visibly grimy. There were a number of women among them who also carried a rough aspect. The Vagarmen wore furs in the Aelbrond custom but their garments consisted entirely of wolf fur. It was rumored that they would journey into the forest without clothes or weapons and come back wearing the furs of wolves they had fought to the death. Some wore pieces of chainmail, but they functioned to join their furs together rather than to offer any real protection. They wore the steel axe pendant of Aelbrond to indicate they had taken the same oaths as the Guards of Lourn. For weaponry they either brandished a two-hander broadsword or a great axe. A spiked chain was wrapped twice around the bodies of each of the Vagarmen. It functioned as a belt securing their furs, though it could be whipped off immediately and swung as a weapon, should either hand come off their main armament.

"Push west!" Rænon yelled as the wind whipped over the deck. The piper played, the oarsmen in turn worked to steer the vessel farther along the coast.

"Furl the sails," Rænon ordered to the standing soldiers as the large galley crested tall waves and sped down the slope to meet another. "Keep pushing along the coast. Harden up into the wind!"

The members of the Shattered Shields who served as deck hands quickly handed the sails and secured them to the masts. They were making way towards the shore, borne swiftly by the waves.

Another clap of thunder. This time as the boom trailed off Rænon picked up the sound of a voice. Again, thunder cracked, and there was no mistaking the Ill-speech that echoed through the sky.

"Unvon sends this storm," Rænon said to Kiv grimly.

"I can hear him too," she said.

"Bring the rain, you cunny!" Rænon yelled skyward to the oncoming grey clouds that moved against the wind unnaturally towards the ship.

On cue the rain fell. The west wind picked up and blew them back towards the rocky eastern shore. Rænon could hear the Ill-speech through the wind.

"Unvon would have us impaled on the rocks before we can

slake our swords! Row if you want blood, you dogs!" he yelled to the Vagarmen, who started their own chant that drowned out the piper. They picked up the oar-pace, fighting against the sorcerous wind.

Rænon could see the black beach now, even through the sheets of rain.

"Row if you want to fight, damn you!"

The Vagarmen yelled the chant, grunting against the burden of the oar. The men on deck joined them in the chant, lifting their morale to reach the final stretch to the beach. Harder the wind blew while the rain fell at an angle against them. The bottom bank of rowers and the horses were sitting in water in the bottom of the ship. The wind howled, Unvon's disembodied voice howled, and the Vagarmen howled as well. Rænon gripped the main oar and wrenched it with corded arms. The vessel gained ground against the forces, and then the shallow, upwards-pointed keel with the angled steel ram broke out of the water and up onto black sand. *Wavelord* had landed.

Quickly the soldiers on deck prepared to disembark. The ramps and ropes were thrown out. The lowest bank of rowers brought the horses on deck and led them down to the shallow water. Rænon took Hyrandi by the reins and led her up onto the black sand beach. Kiv had picked one of Hyrk's horses from his personal stable, a sleek russet stallion. She mounted it and placed an extra bow and quiver on its saddle behind her. Once *Wavelord* was anchored and the Shattered Shields stood on the stormy beach, they waited for Rænon's command.

"Follow behind our horses, and try to keep pace," Rænon shouted through the downpour. "We will head south until we reach a valley, then go east until we reach Shar-kut." The Shattered Shields in unison stomped hard on the shore and replied with the customary "oough."

The small army ran through Unvon's storm, through the blasted obsidian rock landscape. The wind and rain hammered them, but the thought that they would soon reach he who sent the storm drove them onward. They reached the valley within a few hours.

In the valley the black stone had given way to patches of ashen limestone, but the obsidian was always present somewhere within eyeshot. At the base of the valley a small stream was flowing quickly on account of the storm. The Vagarmen were becoming visibly primed for the battle that they could smell was close. Lightning shot down beside the long line of soldiers but they howled in delight. The thunder shook the ground but it only made their war-lust more intense. Soon the tops of the strange towers of Shar-kut were visible and the skies began to clear over the city.

Once the whole of the citadel was in sight, Rænon gathered the Vagarmen behind a large outcropping of rock that was behind the defensive wall and slightly above it. From this position they were able to see the scene playing out in the courtyard before the impossibly-built castle.

On the marble flagstones that surrounded the immense fountain were burnt staves with charred forms tied to them. Living Adyrtun soldiers were bound to other staves. The soldiers screamed prayers, or pleas, to the demon-priests who were lighting the fagots bundled up at their feet. The demon-priests ignored their cries, and sent their own pleas in the Ill-speech to the smokey sky.

Then, the inky water of the fountain began to ripple. Rænon noticed there was another platform at the end of the black pool that was nearest the castle. On this platform was another stave. Tied to this one was a Nitaarian soldier who woefully looked on the black waters.

In an instant, a translucent tendril shot out from the surface and coiled around the bound soldier's leg, tightening with such force that it severed the leg with a popping sound. It dragged the detached limb under the water as the pale soldier shrieked. Another tendril broke the surface, followed by at least a dozen more. They grabbed the entire stave, along with the maimed soldier bound to it, and ripped it off the platform. As the Nitaarian was held in the air by the cluster of smooth translucent feelers, a giant diaphanous form rose high out of the ebon water. The monster's tube-like body was lined with innumerable spiny appendages like a worm from blasphemous depths. This was Yadu-Sha, the God of the Fountain.

Yadu-Sha placed the soldier who had been offered to it into its open vertical maw and chewed with an awful sound. It spit the splintered wood and broken Nitaarian form onto the marble floor. It looked upon the cultists with two small, black abyssal eyes as the priests bowed in supplication and shock.

"The gods, they are rejecting their sacrifices. Even *they* have had enough of the cult," Rænon said to Kiv as she looked on in horror at the scene.

He turned back from the outcropping and narrowed his grey eyes on the small force. "Now we strike. We will ride in first and draw the guards from the castle into the courtyard. Then you charge through the gates. Kill every rock-wearing demon and Kynaran you see!"

With that, Rænon kicked Hyrandi into a high gallop, with Kiv speeding quickly up beside him.

He drew the Godblade from its sheath on his back and howled at the gates of Shar-kut with the sword held aloft. The first pair of Nitaarians to meet him were the soldiers at the gate. The one on his left caught an arrow in the face from Kiv as he swung down on his right side, cleaving the other guard in two. He was still in awe of the keenness of the blade.

The demon-priests that were still in the courtyard shrieked at the incoming riders and ran towards the castle, but not before the God of the Fountain could grab one up with its pellucid tentacles. The tendrils retracted into Yadu-sha's mouth, lifting the priest high above the courtyard into the crushing jaws. As before, the lesser-god retched the remains of the acolyte. The heavy gore cracked the slabs of the marble floor with the impact. Slowly Yadu-Sha disappeared back into the bottomless pool.

The Nitaarian axemen that stood guard at the keep's landing came charging down the stairs towards the riders, a few hundred in number. Rænon could see their awful eyes widen as the whole force of howling Vagarmen entered the gate behind him. He grinned at the oncoming *clawed and fanged* as they took in the fullness of the scene. But still they came, obsidian axes raised. They screamed their demonic war-cry as the two forces met with Rænon at the head of the formation.

Stone and steel clanged in showers of sparks. The Shattered Shields were battle-starved. They tore through the first line of Nitaarians by swinging in great arcs that both rent and threw the Nitaarians with the sheer force of their strikes. Rænon stayed astride Hyrandi, chopping down his foes with the Godblade. Quite suddenly he found that the hard obsidian armor did stop the blade, but if he avoided the armor it would cut through flesh like cream. The first two axemen that came at Rænon attempted to flank him, but he wouldn't allow it. He dismounted and lunged at the attacker from the right, swinging Voidcaller in a horizontal arc that cut through the arms, wooden haft and then the neck of the pale demon, sending its head flying. Using his momentum from the attack, Rænon swung around again. He brought the Godblade down in a diagonal descent that rent the next Nitaarian in the crook of the neck and embedded itself in the creature's obsidian breastplate. The Nitaarian screamed and grabbed at the blade, but the sword severed its clawed fingers off clean. Rænon kicked the axe-wielder in the chest, freeing Voidcaller and sending the Nitaarian through the air and onto his back to die on the bloody courtyard.

The early sun shone directly above the melee. Voidcaller flashed as Rænon swung it through the next Adyrtun guard, and another. Sunlight flashed off the blade. Between the attacks he thought he could see something in the glare of his steel. He swung again, horizontally, to decapitate the next Nitaarian. As his sword passed through the neck and emerged out the other side, it flashed again in the sun. In the glare was a face, something terrible, unutterable, but gone in an instant. Rænon dispelled the image from his mind and lost himself again in a primal state of combat.

Another Adyrtun came at Rænon straight on. He stepped aside at the last moment to let it pass and then swung Voidcaller through its back, halving it in two at the waist. Rænon did not wait for any more to attack, he began a chain of slaughter that sent him into a primal dream, *the armor of ire.* He ducked an axe blade and swung upwards, taking the hands off the attacker at the wrist, then as the Adyrtun fell to the ground he plunged the Godblade into its chest. In a fluid motion he took the blade out and swung low to take the leg from the next Nitaarian to charge him. From this maneuver Rænon walked forward with his blade held low to make an upwards swing at the next enemy. He cut the axe-wielder's skullcap off cleanly. The brain was released into the air to hang outside the skull, tethered by nerves.

A group of Adyrtun quickly circled Rænon. The one he faced in the middle suddenly caught an arrow in the neck. It fell to its knees gurgling black blood. The next one on the left fell with an arrow through the eye. Rænon looked behind him for an instant to see Kiv still on horseback at the edge of the fray, surgically killing

Unvon's demon force. Facing the three remaining attackers again, he let the first one swing its stone axe at his waist. He jumped back. With the Nitaarian momentarily recovering for another swing, he thrust forward and pierced the Adyrtun through the gut. The other two attacked at once, forcing Rænon to take another step back to avoid the two descending axes. As both stone axes struck the courtyard floor they chipped and sent small shards through the air. Rænon with no effort cut the oaken hafts of both axes in two. With a single upwards swing he severed the first Nitaarian's head and took the second one through the shoulder and into the breastplate, which shattered from the blow. *The Godblade is becoming more trenchant,* Rænon thought to himself. He surveyed the fountain courtyard and saw nothing but stacks of black-clad Nitaarians and dark blood covering the marble slabs. The Shattered Shields howled, hunting for any survivors that they might use to satiate their war-lust.

"Into the keep!" Rænon yelled to them. A few of his small army had fallen. He saw one Vagarman with a black axe embedded in his skull. Another on the ground had been set upon by multiple Nitaarians, his chewed face barely recognizable.

"Kiv, take Hyrandi and your stallion and secure them here. We must go on foot. Bring the extra bow."

Quickly she did as she was bidden. They led the Shattered Shields up the giant marble staircase to the great landing before the keep.

"Hold!" Rænon commanded as he looked up at the floating stone slab above the portal to the strange castle. "Don't step under it. Who knows what black oath holds it aloft."

The Vagarmen stepped around the cyclopean stone circle that hovered high in the air. Rænon crossed the threshold into the giant pillared hall. Kiv followed close behind him with a line of Shattered Shields peeling off and following her. Suddenly, without a sound, the stone slab fell fast from its floating position. It hinged on nothing yet fell like a flap, closing the portal tightly and crushing a few of the Vagarmen, leaving gore and limbs hanging from the seam and falling to the smooth obsidian floor. Though this occurrence disturbed his men, Rænon roused them, promising to avenge those who fell. They marched on towards the obsidian pyramid at the end of hall. At the peak of the tall structure Unvon, the master of the citadel, sat upon his throne.

"Who is the helmsman that fought through my storm?" asked Unvon.

"He is Rænon, pyre-smith of the Godblade, hammer of the glowing cult," Kiv shouted to the demonic king.

"Raaaaanon! You are supposed to be dead! Two lying Aelbronders told me they killed you."

"Where are these two?" Rænon asked eagerly.

"I sent them to Kynara, to ride on your lands. Well, *their* lands, I suppose. Though I wish they were here. I would make them regret their lie."

"They think they killed me, so as far as they knew it was no lie," Rænon said while sizing up the room. "It is no matter. I will find them in Kynara after we kill you and the Insane God."

"So you forged the Godblade, and you killed my demon-priest and the Adyrtun I sent to stop you before The Shunned Mount."

"I did."

"And the Adyrtun outside?"

"In pieces."

"I must say, Rænon, as part of the prophecy you do not disappoint."

"I don't care about your prophecy."

"Of course you don't. Aelbronders have always ignored the gods, and the texts."

"We have our god, the dead god Farick who showed us iron."

"Ah, Farick, a lesser-god. Even in death he pesters us with the power in your blade... How I hate steel, and man, and all you've done together. For my tastes the sweetest thing is to see a man who thinks he is victor suddenly become prey. *Ludgaaa shyhd!"* And with Unvon's command his giant Adyrtun commander along with thirty Kynarans in red boiled leather came running up the steps on the far wall behind the throne. The Kynarans carried black stone axes. They did not seem pleased with the situation, but arrayed themselves in front of Unvon's throne.

"These unarmed Kynarans and this mutant are all you have left, isn't it, Unvon?" Rænon said as he held Voidcaller with both hands. Kiv had an arrow nocked, ready to select a target.

"They are all I need. *Adatan tav dai!*" And with Unvon's command the Kynarans lunged forward. Kiv loosed and caught the first man in the throat so that Rænon had the chance to swing. Using the most of his effort he cut through the first two Kynarans with one motion. They fell. Two more fell with the backswing, then another two. Rænon lunged forward and skewered the next man in the gut, then retracted his blade and swung it hard in a flat plane to decapitate a Kynaran with his newly-issued axe raised high. Kiv continued to pick off Kynarans as they charged toward her. The big Adyrtun guard stood below Unvon's cyclopean throne, making sure Rænon could not cut a straight line up to the demon-king.

"Rænon!" Kiv yelled to him through the clamor.

He turned to look. She was still keeping them at bay with rapid fire from her bow, a fluid motion from her quiver to her bowstring, but the soldiers were inching closer. Half the Kynarans were already dead, but she only had two arrows left in her quiver.

"Take it!" he yelled, throwing her the Godblade spinless. She caught it and in one motion hacked through the first straw-haired Kynaran that charged her. Rænon grabbed the newly-forged axe from his belt and entered a frenzied state. Both hands on the haft, he plunged the blade into flesh blindly, retracting it and spinning to cleave into another soldier's chest. Gore sprayed onto the pristine marble flags. Another pair approached him. Now consumed by war-lust, Rænon sprinted at the leftmost soldier and brained him. He swung into the next man's haft, catching the stone blade in his own. Rænon ripped it away from him, throwing it across the throne room floor.

He was the last alive, this Kynaran who traded steel for stone and the promises of the cult. The armor of ire left Rænon as the defenseless Kynaran shuffled back towards the throne where the giant demon guard stood.

"Dok-tysssss," Unvon whispered to his guard, who bent down and palmed the Kynaran's skull. The soldier screamed, his voice broke, then an awful sound and he was silent. The giant guard's hand held a mess of gore and hair.

"That is what you get for fighting for Nitaar, eh Unvon?" Rænon shouted up to the obsidian throne. "That man would've died for you."

"He did." Unvon smiled, showing his blackened fangs. *"Dok-tys!"* The giant guard with the malformed features charged Rænon.

"Take back the sword!" Kiv shouted. She handed him Voidcaller, holding the blade flat so he could grab the hilt. His fingertips felt the hilt just as the towering Adyrtun guard knocked the Godblade into the air and onto the polished stone floor, skidding away. Rænon quickly recovered his axe but the giant guard was fast, knocking him back with a bony elbow to the jaw. Rænon flew, landing on his back. His vision became white and a high pitch stung his ears. He sprung back up just as Unvon's guard brought his polished stone axe down onto the floor, missing Rænon by inches. Now they stood across from one another, each bearing their axe. Rænon would not spare the moment to look away to where the

Godblade landed. He held the demon guard's stare, its eyes a mixture of the commonplace crimson with the gold of high-born demon-priests.

The Adyrtun dropped his shoulder to bring his axe around. Rænon could see its intention, and so swung his axe into the giant's leg. It howled. Rænon took the blade out, let the weight of the axe naturally swing down and back up for him to embed the blade in the guard's skull.

Unvon hissed. He was now alone in the pillared throne room as Rænon kicked the Adyrtun, dislodging his axe.

Kiv handed him back the Godblade and he replaced it in its sheath. He looked up to Unvon who was sitting curled in a ball on the throne with his back halfway to the pair.

"Where is Brakur?" Rænon demanded.

"And Tafala!" Kiv shouted.

"I will take you to the woman who has both, spare me, I beg you!" Unvon pleaded. "They are down the steps, to the sub-levels and the dungeon."

"Down there?" Rænon pointed his sword towards the dark stairwell on the far wall behind the throne.

"Yessss."

"Come down here."

Unvon crawled down the stairs headfirst, on all fours. Kiv let out a muffled noise of unsettlement as the king bent crookedly, moving his clawed hands and feet rapidly in an unnatural way, and reached the floor within seconds. Unvon stood meekly before Rænon.

"Lift the door," Rænon said, moving around to Unvon's back and prodding him forward with the axe.

Kiv was gathering arrows from the dead, filling up two quivers. If Tafala still lived, she could use them.

"Please don't deliver me to them, the barbarian Vagarmen," Unvon begged.

"They listen to my command; I will tell them not to kill you. Now lift the door."

Unvon reached out his pale, black-clawed hand and turned it in the air, muttering something guttural in the Ill-speech. The door silently began to slowly move outwards toward the courtyard as if there were a cushion of air between the massive stone and the portal in which it sat. Unvon then flicked his hand, making a clacking sound with his claws and the slab shot up quickly to its hanging position above the castle landing.

The Shattered Shields rushed forward. "Halt!" Rænon yelled and they stopped with their blades held out at Unvon. Some were mere inches away.

"Take him back to the ship. We need to sail back up to Kynara quickly, but there is still one thing I need to do. Run hard and I will catch up with you on the way back. And bind this one's hands, and mouth… and while we're at it, blindfold him. Watch him closely, he is a black sorcerer." Rænon kicked Unvon toward the Vagarmen. One of the bigger men bent down to tie Unvon's hands.

"I'll take Hyrandi." Rænon held out his hand for the reins as Kiv walked over to him with both horses.

"I'm going with you," she said.

"Very well." They both walked with the horses back towards the throne room. Rænon looked back to the courtyard. The Vagarmen had already roped Unvon's hands and mouth and bagged his face. They were carrying him over-shoulder as they ran out through the gate and back towards the coast.

Chapter XIII

The Meeting

Hooves clapped the marble and obsidian inlays. The sound rang loud and reverberated through the huge empty hall. Rænon and Kiv tied the horses to the black stone sconce at the top of a stairwell that led down into darkness. Rænon unsheathed the Godblade and led the way down, into the black.

A dim ocher light flickered against the wall. Rænon rounded the corner of the massive spiraling staircase. Kiv caught up with him as he stopped suddenly, waiting to hear a sound from below. Only the flickering of flames could faintly be heard at first. Then a low roar, the sound of clinking chains.

"Rænon! Please be a guest in my hall... do not fear... shhht!" The clinking of chains sounded again, followed by faint cries.

"Tafala!" yelled Kiv.

"Kiv! Don't come down here, she controls Brakur, it's..." then her voice was choked off, replaced by the sound of chains.

"Rænon, do not listen to her. We need to talk, come down so I can see you," Narila said softly, almost sweetly.

Rænon slowly rounded the corner with Voidcaller held out, both his hands on the hilt. The immense underground hall was a cavern. Pillars, like the ones above in the throne room and around the fountain outside, adorned the hall. They shined azure and emerald in the light from small pits of flame. The floor was chiseled to perfection and the dark flags were polished to shine in the dim firelight. There were carvings of giant abominations on the walls, runes of Ill-speech and black incantations, and greater, more grotesque monstrosities who seemed to hold sway over the lesser ones carved into the cavern fresco. Many of the calcified fangs of the cavern, either hanging from the ceiling or jutting up from the floor, had been hewn into sculptures similar to those around the fountain outside, unutterable forms of cosmic malevolence and dark powers of creation. There were piles of skulls—skulls of men, Nitaarians, demons, arch-demons. It was a place of black sacrifice and death. In the middle of it, Narila sat on a hewn marble throne in all her glory. Her chosen attire was only a thin chain of silver and nothing else. She stared at Rænon, not with the malice he expected, but an affectionate stare that he could not quite read. Something was different in her face. One of her eyes was now the color of his own.

Tethered to the throne by a chain was Tafala. The archer's arms were bound behind her back. She was kneeling, stripped naked, and bore small cuts and blue bruises all over.

"I gave her pleasure, and then I took some away, then I gave it again. But it hasn't been so bad, has it my pet?" Narila said as she tugged the chain, pulling the archer back on the dark flags before the throne. Tafala spat at Narila, who wiped it off her chest and back into the archer's hair. "These Nitaarians are awful hosts. They have given me nothing but this sub-hall to call my own, nothing to entertain me until *this one* arrived. Now listen, I have an offer for you."

Kiv remained unobserved in the shadows of the stairwell, her bow half-cocked and arrow trained on Narila.

Rænon took a step forward. "An offer from you? The one that pulled me into this fight back on Isahin… I wandered into your den… then found myself on your altar while you attempted to pierce me with my own sword. You loose The Starless Night to feed on Vyntane and bring the Insane God here… I should've made sure I had finished the deed for the vileness of your aims." Rænon spoke venomously. "You know why I am here. Where is Brakur?"

"He is here. For now, I have kept him fixated on me, in a form suitable for this occasion. Regardless of how you feel about us, you cannot win against the Arhai. They are now over twenty thousand strong, you have no chance against them. My offer is that you join us. Win the favor of the Arhai, and the gods, and they will make you deathless."

"Would their favor not sentence me? An eternity of forced company with these fanatics, trapped like Brakur? No, it would not suit me. Besides I am looking forward to the battle."

"Well… there really is nothing I can offer you, it seems."

"No, nothing at all. Now where is Brakur?"

"What about Balan and Murk? I will have them executed for you."

"I will execute them myself. Quit your stalling and summon it."

"Very well, for my eye, I will do it and watch him crunch your bones." Her bare form glistened with dank humidity in the ocher light. She didn't bother to stand as she intoned the arcane words: *"Lixt kun, lixt sannug Brakur!"*

In the deep black shadows of the cavern hall a low, croaking growl sounded. Rænon held the Godblade firmly, his iron form tensed like a viper ready to strike. The dim light from the pits of burning ichor shone on something moving in the dark. Forward it came, slowly. Two eyes of white fire burned brightly in the black. As it came closer the eyes illuminated the crimson visage. A scaled wyrm, with a crest of spikes and long black fangs, stepped forward into the light. It was winged and legless, slithering between the columns of aqua stone, keeping the taloned, leathery wings folded to itself.

Again the crimson wyrm made the low-pitched growl, and then suddenly it made a different sound, terrible and booming—the sound of legions screaming. It shook the sub-hall. As it screamed the wyrm swung its head through a column then back again, bashing its head upon the floor. The wyrm ceased its wailing for a moment, then shot forward to Narila, opening its jaws wide and descending upon her as if to snatch her up from the throne in its ravening maw.

"Lixt kun, lixt sannug BRAKUR!" Narila yelled the incantation again. It stopped right above her head. The wyrm's wide jaws closed slowly, inches from her pate. Brakur retracted its head and focused again on Rænon. The god was under the wafer-thin influence of Narila. Rænon knew she was trying her hardest to control the god in the state it was in, at least for long enough to kill him

and destroy the Godblade.

Threateningly Brakur unfolded its giant taloned wings behind the throne. Narila pointed at Rænon and in the Ill-speech whispered, *"shygval."*

Brakur slid around the throne quickly, using its wings like arms to stand high above the floor. Rænon stayed crouched with Voidcaller poised above his shoulder line. The god descended upon him. As Brakur brought its fanged trap down on Rænon, he quickly dodged at the last moment and now was kneeling under the wyrm's neck. He swung his sword as quick as he could while Brakur was in reach, catching a piece of flesh from the neck and slicing it cleanly off. Voidcaller was still trenchant after the fight outside, for it pierced through the tough crimson scales with almost no resistance. Brakur wailed again, and swung its head at Rænon, knocking him across the floor. He recovered immediately and ran straight at Brakur, who was dripping black blood from the wound in its neck. The wyrm roared and lunged forward. Rænon leapt with the Godblade cocked over his head with both hands. As the open jaws rushed towards him, he struck for Brakur's mouth. Many of the wyrm's black fangs went flying through the air and Brakur wailed again. This time it wasn't the sound of the wyrm, but the sound of thousands of souls sharing the nightmare of a god driven mad.

Brakur looked down at Narila on the hewn throne. She had pulled Tafala close against her bosom. She kept the chain wrapped around her slave's neck, just tightly enough to not quite cut off her breath. *"Shygval!"* she commanded Brakur again.

Just then, Kiv stepped out from the shadows and fired a steel-shaft bolt at Brakur. The arrow deflected off the hard scales and produced a shower of sparks as if it had hit stone. Brakur turned to the archer, who now looked on with panic at the god who opened his broken-fanged jaws and rushed towards her.

This gave Rænon the opportunity he needed. As Brakur slithered toward Kiv, he jumped on the wyrm's back and ran up it towards the head. The Insane God reared its neck sharply upwards in an attempt to shake the Aelbronder off. Rænon slid backwards down its long neck, and while he had the chance, sliced off the wing at the base. This sent a spasm through the wyrm which threw him high into the air. He flew far and bashed against a pillar, sliding down it and landing hard on the base. He was dazed but still rose to his feet as Brakur turned towards him once more.

The wyrm was coming into focus through his blurry vision. It approached slowly as its black ichorous blood spilled from the wing-stump onto the polished floor. Rænon shook his head, trying to regain his wits. Brakur's glowing white eyes fixed on him. It opened its jaws to catch the barbarian with broken fangs. At the moment when the giant maw was within reach, Rænon swung the Godblade in a descending arc which cleaved through the upper jaw between the nostrils and down through the bottom jaw. Dark blood sprayed from the wound as Brakur reared its head and wailed its awful wail through a quartered face. Rænon read the wyrm's movements and could tell Brakur was about to bring his head down upon him in a crushing blow. Rænon knelt with Voidcaller's pommel on the marble flags and its point positioned towards the ceiling.

Brakur slammed down its head in an attempt to crush Rænon with its ruined face, but again the Aelbronder dodged at the last moment and held his sword steady. The point went through Brakur's bottom jaw and stabbed through between the eyes. Brakur let out a weak roar as it raised its head off the floor. Rænon held tight the hilt as the blade slid out of the worm's rising head and then Brakur stopped. The black blood spilled in thick streams to the floor. It looked at Rænon with slightly dimming white eyes. Rænon could tell what the god asked of him. He climbed on its back and onto the horizontal neck just below the base of the skull.

"Stop!" Narila yelled up to Rænon. He and Brakur both turned their heads to the throne and saw Narila holding a dagger to Tafala's throat. The wyrm roared at her weakly, its blood leaving rapidly from the wounds.

An arrow cut through the still and embedded in Narila's forehead, inches from Tafala's face. Narila dropped the dagger and fell limp in the throne as Kiv ran towards her. Teary-eyed she embraced Tafala, holding her weak body and working on the chains that bound her wrists behind her.

"I knew you'd come," Tafala whispered to her friend. "After I saw you kill Vaski I knew you'd find me."

Rænon focused again on the task. He held the sword aloft and swiftly drove the Godblade down into the wyrm's skull. The head, with Rænon on top, fell to the floor. He rolled off before the impact and left Voidcaller embedded where it was. Brakur's white-fire eyes dimmed as did the crimson color of its body. The darkness of a starless night took over the form until the only features were the two dimly glowing eyes. The outline of the wyrm started to fade. The black visage with the faintly luminescent eyes now began to dim as well. Rænon could see the Godblade now, floating above the sub-hall floor as it stayed fast in the fading god's form. He walked over to it. The sword fell from the air as Brakur disappeared. Rænon snatched it by the hilt before Voidcaller hit the floor. He observed the blade.

The dark blood of Brakur had stayed on the sword. It seemed to be seeping into the steel. Rænon held it up closer to the light as all the sanguine substance entered the blade. He could feel its weight was heavier than before. He walked over to the archers who were still embracing each other on the throne.

Rænon flicked Voidcaller and cut the chain that tethered Tafala. The blade was now sharp enough to cut steel with minimal effort.

"It would be unfair to bring this blade into battle," he said, holding it close to his face and admiring the edge.

Chapter XIV

Demon's Wind

The horses rode through the mass of broken forms in the courtyard, away from the fountain and out of the gates of Shar-Kut. Hyrandi paced hard out of the valley and into the blasted obsidian landscape. Kiv followed him, riding her stallion with Tafala seated behind her, holding her arms weakly around her waist. Never slowing down until they could see the ocean, they reached the Shattered Shields as the last of the line met the black strand.

"Take Unvon and bind him to the prow," Rænon ordered the Vagarmen. Already half of them had boarded *Wavelord.* In preparation they had pushed off the sandbar and laid anchor in slightly deeper water. The day was now windless, and the sea was still. Rænon had hoped for different conditions so he could save his manpower for the battle and rely on the wind to carry them north to Kynara. But he had saved a plan.

They had all boarded the vessel and now laid out long planks that reached the shallows so the horses could be loaded into the lower deck. The cold water invigorated Tafala, snapping her out of her pain and lethargy. She was able to pull herself up the ladder and onto the deck. She was still naked from her ordeal. Immediately some of the Vagarmen stripped off pieces of wolf fur and held them out to her. Tafala stood for a moment observing the wild men and women of northeast Aelbrond, who themselves stood mostly naked and stained with black Nitaarian blood. "Rænon, are these the Shattered Shields?" Tafala asked.

"They are," he replied.

She grabbed a piece of fur from a tall man who held it out close for her to take. She held it up to her bosom as if the scrap could cover it. She smiled at him. "What do I care if I wear fur or naught? I will charge into battle with you, shieldless, with no armor but that of my ire and all the arrows I can carry."

The Vagarmen roared and stomped the deck, finding her statement most honorable. Rænon and Kiv smiled to each other.

Rænon marched toward the stem of the ship. Unvon had been bound to the steel-reinforced curved prow of the massive vessel. His feet dangled above an iron ram, fitted with curved horns that jutted out like giant steel spears. His face was still bagged. Rænon ripped off the bag and cut the blindfold. A piece of bloody fur had been stuffed in Unvon's mouth. Rænon grabbed it away, and Unvon snapped at his fingers. Rænon laughed at the demon king.

"I need one of your storms, Unvon. We don't have time to row to Kynara, now send one of your demon winds to our sails," Rænon ordered.

"Why would I do that? Anyway they will not come. They hate the godless barbarians who offer them nothing."

"We are not godless; our god is right here." Rænon tapped his sword. "Always close to us." Rænon put the tip of Voidcaller up to the black-veined neck of Unvon. "Now do your summoning. I've already seen your gods turn on you once."

"I won't," Unvon spat.

"You will, Unvon. You know why? Because you're a cunny, and more than anything you don't want to die—which will happen in moments if I don't hear the Ill-speech." He pushed the blade slightly against the pallid neck and drew a trickle of blood.

"Olluu kulvvvv, olllluuu sudinsu dryr kulvvvv..." The demon king continued to mutter lowly the incantation as the small army stood motionless and quiet on the deck. For moments there was nothing. Rænon could hear only Unvon's voice and the creaking of the ship's wooden planks.

Just then, a faint wind kissed the hairs on Rænon's arms. It picked up slightly, a cool wind that fluttered the sails. Unvon could still be heard at the prow making black pleas to lesser-gods. The wind now picked up to fill the sails.

"Pull the anchor, bank the oars!" Rænon yelled across the deck. The Vagarmen crew moved quickly at his command.

Wavelord sprinted from the beach and into open sea. Unvon had stopped his incantation but still the wind blew at their backs, and still a voice could be heard. It was a voice carried by the wind, guttural and menacing. The words sounded like curses in the Ill-speech. It drove them fast over the still waters, creating rough seas behind them. But the waters ahead remained calm as they were before Unvon began his invocation.

Wavelord cleaved through the Arginese. Rænon had never seen a vessel travel so rapidly. Most of the Vagarmen stayed below deck. They were wary of such powers and hated the Arhai, but said nothing. They knew the demon-wind would save them precious time, and being in the front lines was the priority of the Shattered Shields.

"If this ill-wind stays at our back, we should make Kynara before morning," Rænon said to the archers who stood next to him at the stern while he helmed the vessel. Kiv and Tafala had both donned giant bear furs. The wind still howled with low-pitched voices, fading and then coming closer as the gale whipped at their backs. Still *Wavelord* picked up speed.

"If we keep gaining speed, Rænon, we will be there in hours," Kiv said while holding Tafala tight.

"I hope we do not reach Kynara too soon," Tafala whispered.

"Eh? Why's that?" asked Rænon.

"Some of us might die in the forthcoming battle," she said. "Perhaps all of us. If we must die, it should be without regrets. I do not want to spend what could be my last night alive pining over unfulfilled desires."

"I'm not sure what you're getting at," said Rænon.

"Kiv and I are in agreement…"

Tafala moved towards Rænon and stood close behind him. He realized she was naked under the fur. Her massive breasts pressed against his iron back, her hands moved down to his loins. Kiv approached him from the front and dropped the fur that she had draped over herself. Her skin took on the hue of the sunset and she pressed herself against his chest. She stretched her arms around him to caress Tafala's hips, and then both archers kissed Rænon. The pair took his hand and led him below the deck. Rænon handed the closest man the main oar, pointing his finger north. He could not offer more articulate instructions, for he kept his eyes focused on the nude forms of the archers leading the way down.

The sun was halved by the horizon and all three moons rose in a straight line. A rare omen, the battle omen.

For hours they had sped across the Arginese, cleaving through the night. After midnight the wind seemed to be ceasing. The unnamable voices also died off with the wind. The entire crew had resigned below deck. Rænon had brought a few barrels of ale for the Vagarmen. They were in the bottom two decks, already feasting on the dried meats they had brought.

"Finish up and man the oars! We've lost the wind but we must be close. Row north!" Rænon shouted to his small force below. "And bag Unvon again. If the winds are gone he has no reason to speak."

The piper started his rhythmic tune, and the oars began driving the vessel straight on towards the northern coast of Kynara. All the oars were manned. They had only lost ten men on Nitaar, which gave Rænon even more confidence in the Vagarmen.

The light of the battle moons lit the sea and the sky so that even the far horizon could be faintly seen. Far off to the north small lights appeared. The dark outlines of large ships became larger as *Wavelord* closed in and tall masts stabbed up from the horizon. The piper played his steady tune and the oarsmen rowed without foul. Soon Rænon could see a large force of forty or more ships. As they came closer into view, he could spot the giant Aelbrond galleys flying the axen banner, along with the smaller, speedier crafts from Larion and The Red Jewel. He emptied the horn of strong ale at his side and looked to Haxra, the tall Vagarman that carried Unvon on his back from Shar-kut back to the beach. He was standing on deck awaiting Rænon's order. Haxra was becoming the leader of the leaderless army whether he knew it or not.

"Take the helm, Haxra. Keep it straight on to that fleet," Rænon said. He handed Haxra the main oar and walked across the deck to the bow. He approached the bound demon-wizard.

"Unvon, you can't see it, but we are close. Soon we will join our fleet, and then our force will meet yours. And although you tried to hide down in the Ill-lands, you will play your part in this battle."

Unvon's muffled voice struggled through the black cloth bag and bloody rags in his mouth.

Chapter XV

Banners of Arhai

King Hyrk and Rænon stood on the deck of the king's ship, *The Basyndon.* "More than any other men, I am wary of those that desire eternity," Hyrk said.

"And why?" Rænon asked, almost rhetorically.

"Because they will do anything to get it. Look at them now: fearful, morally limitless," Hyrk said as his eyes reflected the flames.

On the red strand of Sish burned hundreds of fires, hundreds of people. Flames lit up the night and sent thick smoke towards the stars.

"They are burning each other. These demon-priests are ravenous for sacrifice. Desperate for favor," Hyrk said through his teeth. "They would bring the lesser-gods upon us."

"On Nitaar, I saw one of their gods, Yadu-sha." Rænon shook his head as he spoke. "I don't think the gods can always be won by the cult."

"Gods or not, we will see. We cannot waste any more time. Prepare to attack."

"Guards, ready the oars!" Rænon commanded from the foredeck.

The Basyndon was anchored next to *Wavelord.* Hyrk's ship carried three hundred Guards of Lourn, whom Rænon commanded along with the Shattered Shields aboard his ship. These two ships, the biggest in Aelbrond's fleet, were positioned in front of three more lines of vessels, each line containing fifteen ships. The fleet was close enough to the shore that the activities of the Arhai on the beach could be seen. Beyond the red shore was the wall of Sish, and beyond the wall, the great pined city of Kynara.

The Arhai had been caught off guard by Aelbrond's fleet. They planned to march north on the morrow, crossing the Bruna and assailing Aelbrond town by town on the way to Maehlin. Now, all of a sudden they were under siege from the sea and from the north with Utrok's Lanakian riders and the Lourn Guard horsemen camped outside the north wall. The advantage was still theirs, outnumbering Aelbrond more than two to one, but if they failed to repel Aelbrond with their armies on the shore and outside the northern facing wall, then Sish would lay open to the invaders.

Rænon viewed the city from the shore. The smoke rising from the north, beyond the city wall, made it clear to him that the Arhai were still trying to summon aid from the outside. For perhaps a demon's aid, a dark god's favor, the smoke continued to rise into the early morning sky. The smell of burnt flesh made its way to the ships offshore.

As the crews readied the oar banks and began to untie *The Basyndon* from *Wavelord,* Hyrk asked Rænon, "How many you think are outside the wall?"

"Ten... fifteen thousand," Rænon said uncertainly. "Looks

like seven thousand in front of us on shore, so perhaps it's the same on the northern side for Utrok."

"In this fleet behind us we have five thousand men, another five with Utrok. Do you still feel confident?" Hyrk asked him.

"Look on shore, my king. They are dancing around the burning bodies of Sish's own citizens. Our men below are filing their teeth," Rænon said, walking toward *Wavelord.*

Hyrk grinned and nodded in agreement. "See you in the fray, Rænon."

T*he Basyndon* and *Wavelord* were untied and the oars began the beat towards shore. Behind them the other lines in the fleet started to row forward as well. The giant galleys in Aelbrond's fleet held the thousand or so fighters that came from all over the land: Wilaken, Duna, Narav, and other towns from the south and east. Some even came from Haiklan, the ones who would not kneel to the Arhai and escaped into Aelbrond. They carried axes, swords, some were armed only with chains and a belt dagger. Those from the north tended to be pale-skinned, but dark of hair and eye. The men from Duna and Tyluvu were dark-skinned with eyes like the azure waters of the eastern coast. The Aelbrond ships also carried the well-trained infantry of the Guards of Lourn. They wore the characteristic steel armor of the guild, intricately carved and embellished with the ancient battle scenes and runes of Aelbrond. Each man wore a cuirass, spiked gauntlets and a steel helm. Most of them carried shields, and all of them carried swords pyre-forged and blood-tempered.

The only archers to storm the coast came from Larion and The Red Jewel. Their small, sleek crafts carried another two thousand sun-worn giant men, all carrying oaken bows and broadswords.

The flames of sacrifice started to wane as the ships moved in. The Banners of Arhai, slate-colored flags with the open eye of The Watcher emblazoned on one side and the sleeping eye on the other, were waving with the light wind on the red sand beach.

Quickly, the Arhai forces arrayed in lines. The sand continued far back until the dense forest started and the large rock wall rose up out of it. The broad beach allowed for many lines of infantry to form and attempt to force the raiders back into the sea from which they came.

The Arhai had no manned fleet, as the mareships from Haiklan had emptied to bolster the main infantry force. Now consolidated on the shore, this force consisted of the Adyrtun from Nitaar, Kynara's crimson-clad army, and the small force of a thousand from the east in Sarinuk and Yit. They wore thin, ornately carved brass armor that was horned at the shoulders, and brandished long, curved swords of considerable weight.

There were no horsemen, only the talix riders from the east. The saddled reptilians were positioned in the rear, behind all the foot soldiers. The scales of the massive beasts were mostly brightly colored, though assorted black spots and a dark underbelly contrasted with these. They were not overly quick, but well known for barreling fearlessly through the battle line. The creatures had rows of short teeth set in a wide maw that dripped toxic slaver. They were reined by the mystics from the Kynaran Desert, a vast expanse of sorcery and ancient malignancy.

Aboard *The Basyndon,* one of Hyrk's guards stepped up to the giant war horn that stood mounted to the prow. He blew it and it echoed loudly over the waters, up to the city and beyond it for Utrok to hear. This was the signal for Utrok to begin his attack on the northern wall of Sish, so both forces could synchronize their strike. He blew it once more.

The strand was long, and so the fleet spread out far enough that the armies on the beach could not outflank them. The smaller ships from The Red Jewel and Larion came up beside *Wavelord* in a long line as to cover the farthest stretches of Arhai lines. The archers were positioned on deck. They dipped their arrows in lighted pitch and waited for Rænon's command.

The blue dawn was coming. All Rænon could hear through the still air was the sound of small waves lapping the hull and creaking bows. Kiv and Tafala stood next to him with their bowstrings pulled tight, awaiting his word. He closed his eyes to relish the sound of it... "Loose." The archers from the Western Isles fired their lighted arrows into the beachhead.

The din of screaming echoed across the water back to the ships. The archers nocked again. "Fire!" ordered Rænon, and another volley was sent into the lines.

Now Hyrk's ship and the other Aelbrond vessels started to row forward, overtaking the smaller crafts and leading the charge. *Wavelord* stayed out in front of the line. The Vagarmen had worked themselves into a frenzy. They howled as they rowed, frothing for the chance to do battle.

The Arhai returned fire back into the line of ships. Some arrows found their targets on the decks of the Western Isle vessels, but still the archers fired into the beach relentlessly.

Wavelord landed first. The Shattered Shields on deck jumped into the shallow water and the rowers below ran up and jumped overboard, screaming for battle. The Arhai formation did not funnel towards the Vagarmen, instead they awaited their landfall with discipline. Thus they would not leave a void that the other landing ships would soon fill with Aelbronders.

The other galleys landed. *The Basyndon,* with the largest number of Lourn Guards, emptied onto the beach. The Shattered Shields were the first to meet the Arhai. Steel clanged as Rænon and the Vagarmen slashed through the first line of crimson-clad Kynarans. The Godblade cut through steel, boiled leather and flesh all the same. Rænon swung through one man and then through another as he recovered his swing. The Kynarans fell in shock as they encountered the blade.

Another line came and Rænon cut through them, and another rushed forward to meet the same fate, dismembered and maimed cleanly by the trenchant blade. He looked to his sides. The

Vagarmen were slaughtering the Kynarans and Adyrtun that made up the main force on the shore. The obsidian blades and armor were shattered by the cold steel battle axes of the Vagarmen, and so the clawed and fanged Adyrtun were resorting to their demonic instincts and jumping at the Shattered Shields, ripping and tearing at them with black claws and tapered fangs. This tactic garnered better results as it took time to peel off the Adyrtun so that they could be smote with blade or axe. And so the Vagarmen adopted the style by biting and tearing at the Adyrtun themselves, as if it were a fight between demon and war-hound.

The Guards of Lourn were fanning out to the farthest stretches of the Arhai lines, meeting the Kynarans and Adyrtun with a disciplined attack. Typically, a fighter from Lourn will trade blows with an attacker until finding his chance to strike at a vulnerable area. Since the Kynarans chose shields for this battle they found worthy opponents in the Guards of Lourn, who were able to strike hard with broadswords until the wooden shields of the Kynarans were splintered and abandoned.

The Kynarans chose heavy, single edged swords that had a big belly and put much of the weight towards the point, giving the weapons a chopping function that forced the Guards either to adopt steel-rimmed shields or abandon them for agility's sake. And so the crimson-clad soldiers were giving the Guards trouble with their heavy one-handed swords which could be swung rapidly, forcing the opponent into constant defense. The red-clad Kynarans were pushing back on the Aelbronders, but not enough to stop their overall advance.

The section of Arhai soldiers that met Rænon and the Vagarmen had been almost entirely decimated. Now the talix riders started moving from the tree line down to the beach. The archers from Larion and The Jewel had all made it ashore and were firing close range at the sword-wielding crimson soldiers and the Adyrtun who rushed in with black stone axes.

The small group of archers behind Rænon loosed their missiles upon the talix, which lumbered forward on short, thick legs, hissing and drooling venom. Kiv and Tafala had made it to the front line and were both firing into the head of the talix which strode forth in their direction. Finally it fell with no less than forty arrows. Its rider was set upon immediately by Haxra, who took the Kynaran mystic's head off cleanly.

Now the other talix on either side came forward to meet the Shattered Shields, who had penetrated farther up the shore than the other lines of Aelbrond's force. Rænon turned in time to see the talix on his right snatch up a distracted Vagarman who was busy taking on two Kynarans at once. The talix threw him in the air and then caught him again in its vice-like jaws. As he shrieked it crushed him and then swallowed him whole. The talix continued to move toward Rænon and his men, but it had drawn the attention of the other close by Vagarmen who immediately set upon the giant beast ferociously. They hacked at its legs, which forced it to turn and rear. The red-robed Kynaran rider spilled to the sand and was immediately run through. They continued to smite the creature with heavy axes until one of them ran under the talix with his sword low and then swung into the throat, spilling green ichor onto the crimson sands.

The remaining talix on the left had been pierced with arrows but still came towards Rænon. Sparing no instant, he charged at the legged serpent with Voidcaller in his right hand, then hefted it over his head as he jumped at the giant reptoid's face. He struck between the eyes and followed through, cleaving all the way to the brain. The talix fell limp on the sand. The rider of the dead beast pointed his spear threateningly at Rænon just as a bloody sword-point suddenly shot through his chest. The sword was pulled back out again and a nude woman covered in blood, one of the Shattered Shields, stepped out from behind the dead spearman as he dropped to the ground. She howled. Rænon gave her a quick grin and turned back to the fray.

The Godblade could not be more keen. After the blood of Brakur had seeped into the steel, the blade seemed glad to be plunged into battle. As Rænon swung the sword it felt as if the weight of the blade followed an invisible track of slaughter and his arm could only follow it. The sword's swath cut through fighter after fighter. His vision tunneled and every step forward meant a man's death. Every strike with the sword was a killing blow that rent both steel and flesh. Rænon's war-lust was absolute as he cut his bloody way through the Kynaran forces. The faces of both men and demon were sculptures of terror as they met their end at the edge of Voidcaller.

The beach was black with Adyrtun blood. Rænon shook free of the battle frenzy as there were no more Kynarans, no more Adyrtun charging at him. He was surrounded by soldiers separated from their limbs, their heads, all of them cut down by the Godblade. He looked up the beach to his left. The Guards of Lourn and the archers from Larion had hemmed in the Kynaran infantry and were closing in on the now outnumbered force to the north. Soon they would be overtaken.

He looked down the beach to the south. The Aelbronders were fighting against a larger force. There were still a dozen or more talix moving in from the tree line and there were fewer archers down the beach to keep them at a distance.

So Rænon charged south down the strand, coming up on a talix lumbering towards the battle. Both beast and rider were unaware of him running behind. He dashed up the creature's tail and onto its back before the rider could prepare a defense. Quickly Rænon sent the man's head flying and threw the carcass down to the sand. He leapt into the saddle and grabbed the reins, which were silver chains connected to two bolts driven into each side of the talix's head. He pulled the creature to the left. It began sprinting to the southern tree line where the other talix waited for their charge.

The Shattered Shields had almost all moved south down the beach to the larger Arhai threat. They had fared well, Rænon thought, for he saw very few dead. He rode straight to a line of Adyrtun axemen. His talix barreled through them, picking one up in its jaws and sending the rest of them broken through the air. The Nitaarian screamed as the talix chewed his body. Head and legs fell down to the sand while it swallowed the torso.

Rænon continued to ride through the back lines of Kynara's forces to send chaos and panic through the ranks of the ill-trained Adyrtun guards. The strategy was working as the back lines began to run amok. His talix picked up soldiers in its wide mouth and launched them. It trampled the dying under its clawed feet. All Rænon had to do was keep the creature trained on the Kynarans, as the beast was taught to attack any man, not to tell the difference between them.

Rænon was keeping an eye out for Balan and Murk. He knew they would be in the red armor of Kynara and it would be difficult to spot them. But if he knew the two traitors well enough, he guessed they'd be in the back of Kynara's lines.

He crashed into another formation of Nitaarian axemen. The Adyrtun were crushed underfoot as Rænon finally reached the end of the Kynaran lines. He pulled hard to the right side towards the waves. He looked back to admire the effect of riding the talix through the formations of his enemies. The battle lines were now in chaos. He knew these were the optimum fighting conditions of the Shattered Shields. Rænon dismounted and kicked the talix. As it took off southward down the beach, he headed back into the fray on foot.

There were a thousand or so Arhai soldiers remaining and the Aelbronders were setting upon them without mercy, though the Adyrtun still clawed furiously through the fray. They swung their black axes swiftly and tore rabidly with black claws. Many Lourn Guards lay on the beach with their necks ripped open. The

Vagarmen were fighting with chains, swinging them wildly, whipping the faces of the pale Adyrtun soldiers and demoralized Kynarans. The fight on the beach to the north had been settled as stacks of Kynaran and Nitaarian corpses lay piled on the sand. The Guards of Lourn and the Western Isle archers moved south to combine their forces and finish the battle.

The talix riders charged at the archers, who had focused much of their fire on the giant reptoids. When a rider was struck by an arrow and knocked off then the talix would run wild. It grabbed up any man close, including Kynarans, and ate them, before eventually retreating back into the forest. And so the goal became to hit the rider and create a wild, hungry talix to harass the back lines.

Rænon continued to cut through the Arhai. Voidcaller sang as it met another sword, inevitably cracking the other man's steel or halving the blade. There were no talix left now, the Adyrtun had been crushed, and only a small band of Kynarans remained who began to surrender to the Aelbronders. The beach had been taken.

Small brawls were breaking out between the Guards of Lourn and the Vagarmen, surely over stolen kills or stepped-on toes, but they remained fair and weaponless.

"Look what I have found hiding in the waves!" The soldiers made a path as King Hyrk, bloody from battle but whole, made his way through them. He kicked a Kynaran in red boiled leather down into the sand before Rænon. The man in the red helm looked up at him.

"Gods," said the Kynaran, who was carrying an Aelbrond sword.

"Balan! I've been looking for you," said Rænon.

"But I killed you."

"Almost, yes." Rænon grinned at him with his new steel teeth. "The neglected edge of your axe didn't bite too deep, but the river... she was unforgiving."

"Please have mercy on me. I would fight and die for Aelbrond. I broke my oath, but let me regain my honor before I die."

"That time has passed. You don't deserve to fight with the Guards of Lourn and I don't think they'd have you. But I will give you more than you deserve, and allow you to die on your feet in single combat. First, where is Murk?"

"He deserted a few nights ago. He probably ran off to the east where he can hide."

"You know, I traveled all the way to Nitaar expecting to find both of you there... perhaps in your own keep, with your own Nitaarian slaves to do your bidding, only to learn you were sent to fight against this rabid army. I'll wager this is not how you saw your betrayal playing out, is it?" Rænon poked him with Voidcaller. The light gesture penetrated Balan's leather armor and the point went into his shoulder, though only deep enough to draw a trickle of blood. Balan jerked his shoulder back and winced.

“Ah yes, this sword,” Rænon said. “Do you know what it is?”

“You forged the Godblade.”

“I did. And the blood of Brakur enriches its steel,” Rænon said as he admired it. Balan dropped his head towards the red sand. He was silent.

“Drop that pyre-forged blade,” Rænon ordered. Balan obeyed. “Even if I disregarded your other crimes, bringing that into battle against us would be reason enough to kill you.” Rænon pointed to a surrendered Kynaran kneeling on the beach under the pointed blades of the Aelbronders. “Hand this traitor your Kynaran blade.” The man relinquished his sword and Rænon threw it to Balan. “You'll fight with that. I won't use Voidcaller against you. Another thing you do not deserve.”

Rænon looked to Hyrk. “King, would you trade me swords for a moment?”

“Aye.” Hyrk handed over his broadsword. It was the weapon Rænon had pyre-forged from Pitkeeper's steel and the remains of Aarna. Hyrk carefully took Voidcaller from his hand. The soldiers stood back.

Balan grabbed the heavy one-handed hilt up off the sand. He took off his red steel helm and threw it down. His light hair fell on his shoulders and he held the curved Kynaran sword down at his side while staring into Rænon's cold grey eyes. Then he charged.

Balan swung the Kynaran blade up at his opponent's face. Rænon deflected the blade away from him and up, leaving Balan's right side unguarded. He swung the broadsword into Balan's side, cutting through the boiled leather into his ribs. Balan screamed and reversed his motion, bringing the Kynaran sword back down with the blunt side striking Rænon in the shoulder. Rænon's arm went dead for a moment. He switched hands to wield the longsword with his left while he waited for the feeling in his right arm to return.

Again Balan swung the heavy sword, this time in a descending arc to Rænon's now weakened right side. Quickly Rænon parried the strike and forced the curved blade into the ground. He held Balan's sword in the sand for a moment, long enough for the traitor to struggle under the force. In a flash Rænon brought the broadsword up, taking Balan in the jaw and slicing through his face. Balan dropped the sword and screamed, holding his face together in his hands. Rænon held the broadsword aloft and then swung hard through Balan's waist, spilling his guts onto the red sand. Now Balan lowered his hands from his ruined face to hold in his bowels. He dropped to his knees and looked up to Rænon. He tried to speak but his mouth was no longer useful. His hands dropped to his sides and he bled and spilled gore onto the crimson sands of Sish. Rænon swung once more, taking Balan's head and sending it into the waves.

He turned away from Balan's headless corpse, which was still kneeling, and walked back to Hyrk. "Thank you, King," Rænon said, handing him back the bloody sword.

"It is I who should thank you, Guard Command," Hyrk replied.

"We need to head up the beach and climb the hill to the north side, to join Utrok in the main force and gain the wall." Rænon sheathed Voidcaller and looked up to the brightening dawn sky. Dark smoke still rose beyond the city wall to the north, and as the soot made a grey pall over Sish he could see uncanny shapes in it, writhing in the sky.

"And fetch Unvon from my ship."

Chapter XVI

A City Turned Pyre

From their vantage at the top of the hill looking down at Sish, Utrok and his warriors could see the many sacrificial fires burning in the encampment before the great stone wall. The Tarsuleans danced around the fires and chanted in the Ill-tongue. The banners of Arhai flew from atop the towering wall. The sky was dark blue and sunless as dawn approached.

Beyond the wall Sish rose up on a hill of rocky red dirt with immense dark pines rising out of it. These woods were the source of the building material used to construct the houses of the city and the expansive keep. Huge and interconnected, the great keep housed the rulers of Kynara, Tarsul and Haiklan as they had gathered their forces in what they had thought was a safe haven.

There were also many large altars of stone and wood dotting the citadel. These carvings were in the images of the unnamable. At their bases were stacks of bloody heads piled high.

The fires also burned inside the walls of the city. The demon-priests crawled around the burnt offerings, waving their clawed hands at the sky as the smoke lingered overhead. There were no citizens left to be seen, only soldiers and the black-clad Nitaarians who offered these sacrifices to bring dark gods down upon the Aelbronders.

Utrok sat atop a great steed, dark as jet and wild-eyed, which had charged into many battles with him. Next to him was Sedyt, sitting proudly upon the white stallion given to him by Utrok. He wore a steel helm and shoulder lames along with a decorated hammered chest plate, and he bore a great longsword, trenchant and light. Sedyt was the first of his kind to ride a steed, and alongside Aelbronders and Lanakians, no less. He was filled with pride before the battle.

Behind them, five thousand battle-starved horsemen from Lanak and Aelbrond eagerly awaited Utrok's order.

The sky was becoming a lighter shade of blue; the sun would show itself soon. From the top of the hill they also had a clear view of the ocean and Aelbrond's fleet that was approaching the shore. Utrok could see the ships from the Western Isles move forward in the formation. They would hear the horn soon.

At the base of the high slope on which they stood was a great field of tall grass. It stretched far before the wall and would be where Kynara's horsemen, the axemen of Haiklan and the riders of Tarsul would meet the wild steel of the east.

Utrok could see the soldiers from Haiklan against the wall with the mounted Tarsuleans and Kynaran riders in front of them. The men were quiet as they awaited the sound of a horn from the fleet.

A faint hollow sound. Again. And off the shore Utrok could see flaming arrows sent to shore.

"Ride!" Utrok yelled. His Lanakians shouted their war-cry,

and the Guards their own. Sedyt, louder than them all, let loose a demonic shriek which strangely heartened the men. Utrok kicked his steed and charged down the slope with Sedyt on his tail and the five thousand horsemen close behind.

Through the pines they sped down the hill as the Kynarans also began their charge. Sedyt gained speed and was right beside Utrok as they met the level field at the hill's base. His red eyes burned, and he continued his piercing howl as he overtook Utrok. He raised his blade high above his head. The sword was one with his pale hand and he loved the steel. Sedyt kicked his white steed again as he led the charge into the Arhai. Arrows sung over his shoulder towards the approaching enemy. He screamed again.

It was a sound like thunder. The two forces clashed on the field with the din of felled horses, singing steel and the cries of men filling the air.

Utrok stacked the slain with his sword. His blade flashed as it found the neck and arteries of his enemies and soon he had cut a large circle of dead men around him. The Aelbronders traded between bow and sword, taking time to keep the enemy at a distance by firing arrows at the concentrated groups of Kynarans and Tarsuleans to thin them out.

The Lanakians fought with brutal force. They shared the Vagarmen's approach to battle, virtually ignoring their own safety and putting up a shower of steel that required constant defense by the enemy. They wore great steel helms, some were riveted with sharp spikes, others featured curved horns that terminated close to one another at the level of the soldier's chin. Those who did not wear shirts of mail were clad in black furs with lames of steel sown on the shoulders and chest. All wielded straight, single-edged swords with a point that was sharply angled from the blade to the spine's tip. These were notoriously thick blades designed for chopping. They also carried wide, double-bladed war axes on their backs, but bore no shields.

Many Lanakians fell on the front line's spears. The Tarsuleans now abandoned the long pikes they carried in favor of their broadswords. Both forces were losing men in the bloodshed, but Kynara's riders were taking a heavier toll. The Guards of Lourn continued to rain arrows on their crimson-clad enemies and would vigilantly watch each other's backs to avoid being taken unaware. They bore long narrow shields to protect themselves from opposing fire, as the Kynarans were also sending arrows from the flanks into the maelstrom of battle.

The Tarsuleans were having trouble breaking through the volley of arrows as the axemen from Haiklan finally made their way into the ruck. The men from the north hacked at both the Lanakians and their horses in a desperate attempt to bring the battle down to the ground. One of them found Utrok in the middle of the fray. The ruler from Lanak wore a famous helm of steel and brass spikes. It covered a portion of his face with a carved visage of the ice-serpent around his dark eyes and broad nose. Any man familiar with his legend could spot him. The axemen swung into Utrok's stallion, cleaving into its chest and splattering blood back onto Utrok himself.

Utrok was overcome with rage. His beloved stallion neighed and fell sharply towards the bloody dirt. The axeman who had slain the horse could see Utrok's wild eyes under his dark helm staring into his own, and they filled him with fear. The giant king crashed onto the northern axeman from his falling horse and knocked him to the ground. Utrok ripped off the man's steel helm and took a moment to savor the Haiklaner's regret before he ruined the man's face with his own helm. Utrok stood up from the bloody pulp and dropped the helm, retrieved his broadsword and engaged with the other axemen from Haiklan as they made their way from the back lines. He continued to carve a bloody path to the wall.

Sedyt swung his lithe blade ferociously, trading blows and also taking a few himself on his helm. The pale, steel-clad demon atop a Lanakian steed sent a shock through the Kynaran horsemen who saw him charging forth. The first of his kind to do so, perhaps the last. He screamed through his sharp teeth as he felt what the Aelbronders called *the armor of ire.* He cursed the Arhai as he clanged swords with them. His narrow, thin blade was finding its way through the leather armor of the Kynarans and the riveted steel plates of the riders from Tarsul. He held a blackened steel shield made for him by Utrok's men and he used it to defend his left side against the enemy, who were now taking notice and starting to rally against him. The Lourn Guards concentrated their fire around Sedyt to stop the unified effort against him. Soon Sedyt was clear of attackers and many ruined corpses lay at his stallions' hooves. He looked back at the Guards of Lourn who saved him and saluted them quickly before riding straight back into the fray.

But one of the Kynaran archers had his eye on the pale rider from Isahin. As Sedyt raised his sword high to take the next man in the neck, an arrow shot through his back and the steel point appeared through his chest. Sedyt coughed black blood and dropped his shield. Again he raised his sword in the air and screamed his demon war-cry. He kicked his white steed into a sprint and rode off hard towards the wall, swinging his steel in bloody arcs as he cut a way through the Kynaran force and made it to the no man's land before the wall. He turned back to view the battle and fell from his white steed to the red dirt, still holding the gift from Utrok in his grip as he died.

Utrok, still in the slaughter-fever, was killing without restraint. He strode forth towards the wall with a small force of mounted archers, who thinned the ranks so he could face one or two enemies at a time. He had cut his way through the battle and now stood in the trampled void before the wall. He looked back to the field to see his men.

The Haiklan infantry had been mostly picked off by the archers from Aelbrond and the Lanakians, who fought mercilessly with their heavy blades. The Tarsuleans still held a majority on the field, as they were behind the Kynarans in the initial charge.

Aelbrond was not without its losses. Many Lanakians and Guards of Lourn lay pierced with arrows, impaled with spears.

Though of the five thousand, still more than four thousand remained. Aelbrond had evened the numbers and now only the Tarsuleans stood between them and the wall.

As Utrok strode back to the battle he heard a horn call. He stopped, listening carefully.

The hollow sound of a warhorn called louder this time as Rænon, Hyrk, and the forces from the beach came roaring up the hill and onto the field.

Kiv and Tafala were already firing arrows at the Tarsuleans who peeled off from the battle and rode towards them.

The Shattered Shields crested the hill, howling and covered in blood both black and red. Most were naked and had sheathed their blades in favor of spiked chains. The Tarsuleans rode at them, then suddenly reared their horses as the archers from Larion and the Jewel also topped the hill. With the mounted archers positioned outside the fray hemming them in, they realized they were running out of retreat routes. Now, with the rabid Vagarmen taking the field, there was mass panic among the riders of Tarsul.

The archers from the Western Isles advanced, taking care to fire at the flanks of the battle and not hit the Lanakians or Lourn Guards still in the fray. The men from the east of Aelbrond, in Duna and Tyluvu, plunged into the ruck, swinging hammers and flails. Rænon and Hyrk fought together. The Godblade cleaved through the maelstrom, tearing through the remaining Kynaran forces that did not drop their swords in surrender. The Shattered Shields ripped their chains through the enemy ranks. The horses were harassed and tossed their riders, and once their feet hit the field the Tarsuleans and remaining Kynarans fell to the ravening iron of Aelbrond.

Now the land and sea outside the wall of Sish had been won. A small force of Tarsuleans had surrendered, a hundred or so men. The axemen from Haiklan had been wiped out by the Guards' mounted archers, and the Kynarans that rode in first had been cut to pieces by the Lanakian riders and their heavy steel.

The smoke still rose black from beyond the high stone walls. As Rænon looked to the sky he could see the uncanny shapes among the clouds. Immense, writhing forms that shifted quickly from an amorphous mass of teeth and ripping claws, to a scaled form that dipped low into the smoke and almost touched the tall wooden keep at the top of the hill.

Unvon stood before the wall, held at dagger-point by Tafala. Chains were wrapped around his head and mouth, leaving only a space for his eyes to see. He tried to speak through the chains, and after looking upon the shapes in the sky for a few moments he began to scream.

"How will we gain the wall?" Hyrk asked Rænon and Utrok. The three stood before the huge black iron gate, wiping the blood from their faces and hands.

"We have no battering ram. I say we stack the slain, climb over it," Utrok suggested without emotion.

"Stack your dead against the gate," Rænon commanded the surrendered Tarsuleans. "Quickly, now, or we will feed you to them." He pointed to the sky. The Tarsuleans began to gather corpses from the field and arrange them in a pile against the wall. When the pile reached the top of the twenty-foot gate, Rænon selected a force of men eager for glory to make the assault.

Rænon led his chosen warriors up the mountain of slain men to the top of the wall. Once over the threshold, arrows from the fortress assailed them. Some Aelbronders fell, but the Western Isle archers came up behind them, returning fire. Soon, so many reached the top that the arrows could not overcome them. They gained the tall gate and Rænon lifted the large steel bar that locked it shut. The gates swung open against the piled bodies stacked next to it and Hyrk led the line into the breach.

Once beyond the wall the Shattered Shields stuck behind Rænon, who sought to gain the hill and the wooden keep where the rulers surely made their lair. They brought Unvon with them in the back.

Kynaran archers fired instantly upon them crossing the gate. Immediately Rænon took an arrow in the left shoulder. He knelt down clutching the end of it. He knew the arrow missed his heart because it pumped hard in his chest, and it missed his lungs because he could yell loudly, "Rip it out!" to the Vagarman, Haxra, behind him. Rænon broke the fletching off. Haxra grabbed the length of arrow that stuck out of his back and ripped it through Rænon's body. Rænon grabbed the broken shaft from him and charged the line of archers before they had time to nock more arrows. He sought the one who had struck him. Upon finding his man, Rænon stabbed the archer through the eye with the steel arrowhead of the broken shaft. A stream of blood flowed from the screaming archer's wound down his chest. Rænon yelled back to his men, "Burn their altars! Burn Sish!"

The Guards of Lourn lit their torches and set the wooden altars ablaze. Already there were sacrificial fires set all over the city. There was nothing left of Sish's populace, everything, everyone, had been offered to the dark gods, and the demon-priests had retreated to the tall pine keep.

The Lourn Guards now surrounded the keep, ready to mount the tall hewn staircase leading up to it. There was one larger idol before the steps of the keep, a massive carved image of a crouching, clawed thing with many eyes. "Do not burn this altar. Bind Unvon to it instead," Rænon ordered the Guards.

The forces continued to funnel through the gate when, from the south, a line of talix rushed around the corner and caught a number of Lourn Guards up in their slavering jaws. The men struck at the reptilian faces as the vice-mouth crushed the life from them and swallowed them whole. Behind the talix were more axemen from Haiklan and the last of Kynara's crimson-clad swordsmen, who came to offer a last stand for the Arhai.

The archers immediately organized around the talix, concentrating their fire on one at a time until the thing fell or turned back. The Lanakians met the Haiklan force straight on, fighting axe for axe in shieldless battle. Rænon sprinted from the idol to the fray, jumping in with the Godblade aloft, rending flesh and mail the same.

The shapes in the sky clamored too with the sounds of battle, the clanging of steel like thunder. In the hanging smoke and roiling clouds something screamed and shook the ground, causing every soldier to cease and cover their ears.

Tendrils shot down from the smoke to the battle and clenched an entire company of Kynarans approaching from the back. It held the hundred or so men, wrapping them with more and more tendrils until they were encased in a translucent sphere. Their screams could be heard as the sphere was pulled up to the sky by rigid, thin, stalky arms. A face shot out from the smoke. As big as a mountainside, the mouth hung open loosely, awfully, and the forehead was full of dead black eyes. The thin, rigidly moving arms delivered the sphere into the hanging mouth. It snapped shut, making a sound like thunder that shook the ground, and the face disappeared back into the thick grey pall. More tendrils reached out for the Kynarans and another hundred or so men were grabbed up by the myriad translucent arms. These men were also rapidly entangled in the sky-borne tendrils. Now it was clear they were being dissolved horribly inside the sphere. Again the face appeared from the smoke and the trapped soldiers were fed to the gaping maw. Panic spread through the rest of Kynaran force.

That is the same face from the idol, Rænon realized. He looked back to Unvon who was chained to it, staring up in horror at the events in the sky. Then he remembered it, the face that appeared in the glare of his steel in the courtyard in Shar-kut, it was this same terrible face.

"Take the keep!" Rænon yelled to the Vagarmen as they directed their attention away from the frantic Kynarans being eaten alive by their own god.

Rænon led the way up the giant stairs to the keep when from under the grand, carved wooden gate at the stair's summit, men ran forth screaming, "Shagr-ot! Shagr-ot!" They flew down the stairs until they saw Rænon and the Shattered Shields. They stopped, frozen in fear of both what lay above and before them. They were the leaders of Kynara's armies. Among them were King Hoxu of Kynara, the usurper King of Tarsul, an Ahrai priest named Dyondam, and the traitorous King Hardboar from Haiklan.

"Bind them all to their idol along with Unvon," Rænon commanded the Vagarmen. "We will leave their fate up to *them.*" He pointed above to the shapes in the smoke. "And burn the keep."

He looked down upon the city aflame, watched the last of the Kynaran soldiers and fleeing demon-priests that were being fed upon by the one they called Shagr-ot.

The four kings and their generals were bound to the giant cyclopean idol as Sish and the great pine keep burned behind them. They pleaded to the Vagarmen who wrapped them with chains. They made dark invocations to the sky as the uncanny shapes appeared in and out of the towering smoke.

Rænon, along with Hyrk, Utrok, Kiv and Tafala, stood at the

gate and watched the city turn pyre with the armies of Aelbrond behind them.

Once more the tendrils shot out from the pillar of smoke, descending upon the city and wrapping the giant idol and the bound kings with it. The idol was quickly enveloped in the translucent arms and wholly wrenched from the ground. The kings shrieked as they dissolved inside. And then, by thin, jointed arms they were delivered to the abyssal maw hanging under the black, lifeless eyes of Shagr-ot.

Hyrk and Rænon boarded *The Basyndon,* each slightly limping. Rænon held his shoulder that had been pierced. The king had been sliced in the leg and forearm but was not in danger of losing either appendage.

"We never discussed what you wanted for this victory, Rænon," the king said as he ripped the cork off a glass of strong balt with his teeth. He handed it to Rænon.

"I haven't given it much thought. I have enjoyed crushing the Arhai, and I forged the Godblade, which is enough for me."

"You must want something. Name it."

"I'll take Runefare, if it's on offer."

"It's yours," the king said without hesitation.

Rænon smiled as he thought of the great stone towers. "All I ask is that you hold it for me until I get back. I'm going east."

"Of course, but for what?"

"The thrill of the hunt."

"Hunting? What will you hunt there?"

"Murk."

ABOUT THE AUTHOR

Jason Christopher Tarpey is a musician and blacksmith from Boerne, Texas. He is the vocalist for Eternal Champion, Iron Age, and Graven Rite. The lyrics of many Eternal Champion songs, such as "I Am the Hammer," "Ravening Iron," and "Banners of Arhai," were based on characters and events that appear in *The Godblade.* His first story, "Vengeance of the Insane God," is a prequel to *The Godblade,* and can be found in the DMR Books anthology *Swords of Steel Omnibus.* Tarpey also operates Hammerhall Forge, where he creates his hand-forged iron works. He would like to thank Matt Doinidus for coming up with the name *Voidcaller.*

ALSO AVAILABLE

Want to get an e-book for free? *The Infernal Bargain and Other Stories* is available exclusively for DMR Books mailing list subscribers. Go to www.DMRBooks.com and get your copy now!

Swords of Steel Omnibus – *Swords of Steel,* with its novel concept of fantasy stories written by members of heavy metal bands, was the most critically-acclaimed sword-and-sorcery anthology series of recent years. Now every story from all three volumes is packaged together! Features Howie Bentley (Cauldron Born), Byron Roberts (Bal-Sagoth), E.C. Hellwell (Manilla Road), Mike Scalzi (Slough Feg), J. Christopher Tarpey (Eternal Champion) and many more.

Karnov, Phantom-Clad Rider of the Cosmic Ice by Matthew Knight, Howie K. Bentley and Byron A. Roberts – Returning from battle, the warrior Karnov discovers his family murdered and his homeland ravaged by vampyres. Aided by witchcraft and sorcerous allies, will Karnov's powers and burning lust for retribution be enough to avenge his loved ones, or will undead wraiths corrupt the earth forever? Classic horror film atmosphere meets pulp-style swashbuckling adventure in this action-packed epic.

The Chronicles of Caylen-Tor by Byron A. Roberts – The Wolf-King of the north, Caylen-Tor, does battle with imperial armies and sorcerous serpent-men in three exciting novellas! Spectacular sword-and-sorcery by the lyricist of Bal-Sagoth.

Lands of the Earthquake by Henry Kuttner/Under a Dim Blue Sun by Howie K. Bentley – The first split release from DMR Books in the tradition of the Ace Double series! *Lands of the Earthquake* is a classic science-fantasy adventure from the pulp era that has never been published in book form before. On the flip side you'll find a brand new sword-and-planet tale. A US soldier hijacks a Nazi spaceship and lands on a planet threatened by snake-men!

Necromancy in Nilztiria by D.M. Ritzlin - The world of Nilztiria is an ancient one. Beneath its brilliant crimson sun and demon-haunted moons wondrous treasures lay buried, waiting to be uncovered by intrepid adventurers. Yet peril abounds as well, in the form of nefarious sorcerers, grotesque beasts, and inexplicable phenomena. If you crave stories of adventure and wonder with a touch of gallows humor, look no further than these thirteen tales of Nilztiria!

Renegade Swords – This anthology contains eight fantastic tales, each of them obscure or overlooked in some way. Includes stories by Robert E. Howard, Clark Ashton Smith, Manly Wade Wellman, and more!

Swordsmen from the Stars by Poul Anderson – Three classic novellas from the pages of *Planet Stories.* Heroic science fantasy at its best!

The Eye of Sounnu by Schuyler Hernstrom – This collection contains all of Hernstrom's critically acclaimed stories for *Cirsova Magazine,* as well as a few uncollected and unpublished tales. Running the gamut from sword-and-sorcery to sci-fi, these heroic adventure stories will satisfy fans of Robert E. Howard and Jack Vance!

The Thief of Forthe and Other Stories by Clifford Ball – After the death of Robert E. Howard, Clifford Ball was the first writer to follow in his footsteps and pen sword and sorcery stories for *Weird Tales.* For the first time ever, all of Ball's stories are collected into one volume. A must-have for pulp historians and fans of fantasy, horror, and weird fiction!

The Sapphire Goddess: The Fantasies of Nictzin Dyalhis – At last, the stories of one of the most unusual writers of weird fiction are collected! This volume contains all of Nictzin Dyalhis' works of fantasy and science fiction, many of which have never before been reprinted. Those who love the wild imagination and masterful prose of authors such as Clark Ashton Smith and C.L. Moore are sure to enjoy this collection.

Death Dealers & Diabolists – Eight action-packed tales of swords and sorcery! Includes stories by Keith Taylor (author of the *Bard* series) and Buzz Dixon (writer for *Thundarr the Barbarian, G.I. Joe* and *Transformers).*

Warlords, Warlocks & Witches – Eight more fantastic tales of action and adventure! Features stories by David C. Smith *(Red Sonja, Oron)* and Geoff Blackwell *(Swords of Steel).*

The Great Die Slow and Other Tales of Dark Adventure by Harry Piper - Set in a Dark Age Celtic landscape shrouded in myth and legend, these dark, often tragic, tales tell stories of ordinary men and women confronted by evil both human and inhuman.

Heroes of Atlantis & Lemuria – Classic tales of adventure from the sunken lands! Includes five Kardios stories by Manly Wade Wellman, all three Lemurian tales by Frederick Arnold Kummer, Jr., and a hard-to-find Leigh Brackett story set in Mu.

The Road to Infinity by Gael DeRoane – Aran Dyfar's wanderlust leads him on a quest to discover the mythical Road to Infinity. Along the way he encounters friends, monsters, and wonders beyond imagination. A picaresque adventure sure to please fans of Jack Vance's *Dying Earth* and *Lyonesse* series.

Printed in Great Britain
by Amazon

59159249R00092